Black Lace
Anthology of Victorian Seduction

By
Eryn Black

Eryn Black

Copyright © 2014 Eryn Black
All rights reserved.
Edited by Cameron Hill
Cover Art by Erin Dameron-Hill

ISBN-13:
978-1497561465

ISBN-10:
1497561469

All rights reserved. No part of this publication may be reproduced in any form without permission from the holder of the Copyright and author.

This book is a work of fiction. Names and characters are a product of the author's imagination. Any resemblances to actual events or persons are coincidental.

Black Lace

This collection

is dedicated to

The woman who taught me to dream and
believe in love.
My mother

Other Books
by
Eryn Black

Sovereign Sinners
The Viscount Returns
The Earls Lady Wife

Black Odyssey
Black Lace
Bound To Her Earl

The Master's Series
Maid For His Submission
Seduced By Her Master
The Master Submits

Tales of Club Odyssey Series
Members Only
Making The Master Beg

Nephilim Wars
Kindred Sacrifice
The Perfect Little Bite
:An Amuse Bouche

Black Lace
:An Anthology Of Victorian Seduction

Eryn Black

Book One
The Dukes Virgin Bride

Book Two
Her Quiet Barron

Book Three
An Affair At The Opera

The Dukes Virgin Bride

Chapter 1

London 1851

Wax pooled around the brass base of the candlestick. Burning in anticipation, the poor little wick was now a shriveled memory of itself... A ghost of a night, now lost and overshadowed with the pains of what could have been, now told in the wax stalactite.

Rolling her head back, Cynthia's neck popped out a chorus of all her pent up tension. He had left her eighteen hours ago and now it seemed there was no hope of his return. The room still echoed from his exit that morning, and now alone and shivering from the growing cold of the night, Cynthia was starting to come to realize that perhaps this was just one of many lonely nights ahead.

It was an arranged marriage that promised her -now absent- Duke a generous payoff from her dowry, while Cynthia was promised a title and marriage in exchange.

Perhaps not such a fair trade now that she saw her new life from the inside out. She had begged her father not to sell her into marriage so quickly; to at least be given a chance to meet her perspective husband before the bans were read. Now, he was a stranger who owned all rights to her body.

...But one month later her maidenhead was still intact.

Stretching her back, she rose from the lounge, abandoning the gothic novel, to cross her cold room and try to stir the embers back to life. A smirk played on her lips, growing from the painful truth that this was the only warmth she might ever feel in this oversized prison cell. Perhaps she was expecting too much. After all, she had only been intended to be his brood mare, meant only to provide him with his heir and a spare. Like any other member of the ton, her husband's passion and warmth was to be saved for his mistress's bed.

Wiping the black soot from her hands over her clean, white nightgown, she straightened and moved to the oversized and unused bed. Intended to be worn for her wedding night, she had been dressed in the same gown and ready every night, awaiting the time that her husband would claim his rights. Loneliness was her blanket this night, as she curled her legs up close over the counterpane and passed the rest of the night as she always did, trying to dream of the love and passion that was foreign to her and would probably remain so.

Drip, drip, drip... The wax kept building its tower, and Cynthia watched hypnotically. Every drop of hot wax fell on top of the last and then ran a trail over the curves that had formed. It all reminded her of perspiration running down her body on a hot summer day. It was calling out to her, taunting her, tempting her for just a little touch... just a little taste of what her body was craving... to feel alive... to feel excited... to just feel.

Catching a drop on her fingers, she winced at the sudden burn, but before she even blinked from the pain, the wax had cooled. The gentle warmth soothed her fingertips. Rubbing her fingers together, she noticed how it was soft and hard all at once. Forming under the pressure of her fingers until it would cool and then crack. Dipping her finger again into the melted wax that pooled under the burning wick, Cynthia flinched from the burn of the hot wax only to retrieve her fingers thickly coated. Hot wax sealed her fingers, and what had been a painful burn, was now growing more and more appetizing. In the burning pain, there was soothing warmth that followed with every dip and drip. Soon temptation took over. Lifting the candlestick, Cynthia tipped the candle over her open palm watching the pearl beads of wax drop.

Drip, Drip, Drip.

It was a charge to her senses, sending tingles up her arm and shooting through her body. Cooling quickly in her hand, the wax made a thin casting of all the crevasses, holding in the heat that pulsed down to her core.

"Oh my!" Her body hummed in the sensation. She was stung with the sharp burning pain once again, but quickly, as before, she could feel the soothing warmth of the wax embrace her and travel down to her core.

Alive with a need for more, she dared to bear more, before propriety caught up with her. Cynthia needed more, and she did not hesitate to unlace the neckline of her nightgown, spreading the delicate linen apart, revealing her round, soft breasts to the cold air of the night. Her nipples hardened to the rush of cold, but she did not shrug back into her nightgown, nor did she shy away from her new found boldness. This was the new Cynthia, the new Duchess, who did not question her needs beneath the good of her Duke. Cynthia felt empowered in her lust and eager to explore the taboo to give her some sense of warmth, some sense of need. She was a living, breathing woman who had never known the pleasure that was contained in her body, and if her husband refused to teach her what she longed to know, then she would explore it on her own.

Holding the candle over her chest, she could feel her resolve shake, knowing that she would have to face the sharp, burning pain before anything else. All of this was new to her, and she questioned whether or not this was something to be attempted. Ladies were not meant to seek physical pleasure, that was left for the husbands and their light skirts to enjoy, but there was no escaping the fact that her body was crying out for more, and whether or not that meant she was not a true Duchess, then so be it.

Tilting her head back, she poured the silky thread over her chest and down the path between her breasts, gasping at the burning pain. She was warmed instantly, and her breasts and nipples ached to be touched. Pressing her hand into the cooling wax, she rubbed the warmth into her while a new vibration began to sing down into her mound.

Hissing from its final drops, the dying candle flame winked goodnight. Only the dying embers from the fireplace were left to chase the shadows back to the corners of the room. Cautiously in the dark, a half dressed intruder worked his way across the room.

Little in his world was denied to the ton, and Charles was among the elite. The privileged life of a Duke was filled to the brim with possibilities and women were no exception. Charles Elroy Debracey, the Fifth

Duke of Chentry, was a prize to any woman who was granted a taste of his pleasures... only they left a bitter taste, for there was only one he craved. He could still smell the exotic aroma from the playrooms at his club on his neck cloth, and his head slightly spun from the absinthe. The Odyssey was known for its more exclusive choice in courtesans and their erotic tricks. Housing the secret erotic pleasures and fantasies of the ton, the Odyssey was without the dark rituals of the Hell Fire club. All of these dark pleasures and temptations he had gotten to sample, and now after a month of imprisoning himself to a vow he made to stay true to his bride, Charles was a starving man.

... His bride? Those two words held so much power over him. How was it that a single woman could hold his future happiness in her delicate body when he had so often taken two sometimes three to his bed at once? Favorite among the sinners of this secret sex club, Charles brought with him a sensual dominance to their beds that few could master. Potential mistresses often approached Charles, but he never had the patience to take on an exclusive lover... not when there were so many to enjoy.

Tonight though, none could satisfy his need. After a dry month of matrimony, he had finally decided to slake his lust and take Odyssey's pride and joy, Paulette, to bed after a luscious demonstration of her bound to the Saint Andrew's cross; but even with her large breasts and heart-shaped lips made to swallow his cock -she could not get a rise out of him. There was only one woman he wanted, but he feared her disgust and resentment when she discovered what it was he craved.

Even now, he could still picture the first glimpse of his bride. Not long before the bans were read, Charles managed to convince his uncle for a glimpse of the woman whose dowry would save his family from ruin. She had been seated at her harp for her daily lesson. Blasted instrument! To this day, he still could not see why every young debutant had to be trained with some musical skill? It was all just noise made to try and beckon a suitor with their mating call. The annoying sound of the twanging strings was almost enough to send him running, but then he saw her. Billowing, deep brown, locks floated down her back. She did not wear her hair up like so many of the debutants did.

White chiffon fell from her shoulders, flowing at her waist and held in form with a crimson ribbon and then fell down to the floor. Cloaked under the shield of innocence, her wild heart was screaming to come out. From the touch of sinful color at her waist, to the ankle that peaked out from under the skirt that had been pulled up to help hold the harp close. Was she accustomed to taking larger instruments between her thighs, or was she truly innocent to the sinful thoughts that she was bringing to his mind?

Before any introduction could be made, Charles was pulled from the house by his uncle and denied the chance to meet his future bride. Their families had to strike a bargain, and his Uncle was determined to play the title as far as he could without his nephew's interference. Self-made commoners such as Cynthia's father were willing to pay what was needed to gain a title for his daughter, and that was what Charles's Uncle had planned on. It was left until their wedding day, standing before the priest, family and few friends, till they were able to meet face to face. Her red, swollen eyes told him what she thought of her new husband, and he had been ashamed of himself ever since.

The only thing that was more of a disaster then their wedding was their wedding night. Charles had planned on biting back his own personal needs for her luscious body and make her sexual introduction a gentle one. If only the road to hell was not paved with good intentions because that is what his wedding night was... Hell.

Over the last month, Charles had spent a few moments to a few hours in his wife's room every night watching her sleep. Brushing back her hair, he pulled the discarded coverlet over her exposed shoulders and snuffed out the burning candles. She had become not just his beautiful duchess, but also an obsession. There was nothing he would deny her, nor was there any harm he would risk on her. That was his tragedy; with his new wife, he was only half a man.

Ashamed for his cowardly behavior that night, he turned from her rumpled bundle curled up in the chair. Hoping that if he had satisfied his beastly needs with the experienced flesh at the club, he could finally take his wife's innocence gently as it should be done. Burning with a need like this, he feared how demanding he would be of her.

A nameless murmur brought his focus back onto his sleeping wife.

Had she said his name? He asked himself. Was it possible that despite her fear for him she might hold some desire for him?

There was no ignoring the black soot marks that tarnished her thin dressing gown. It was clear to him that she had been eager for her privacy tonight and sent away her lady's maid early. A pathetic excuse for a husband, he cursed himself for his actions toward Cynthia since their wedding... or rather his lack of action. If she had sent the servants away for the night, then he should have been nearby to offer her what was needed and been ready to serve her as a worthy husband. Looking toward the dying flames on the hearth, he could see himself kneeling with pride, stirring the embers back to life, and laying fuel to the burn: keeping his wife warm and in comfort. Humbly he would have served her if she wished it. All she needed to do was ask and he would cast aside his own needs in order to please hers.

"Charles."

There it was again? His heart jumped to hear his name floating from her lips.

Brushing her hair away from her face, Charles took in an eyeful of what he had denied himself.

"Enough of this," he cursed. Tormented night after night, it served no use to spend every sleepless hour constantly aroused and ripped apart with longing. Carefully lifting her into his arms, Charles carried her to bed where the covers had already been turned down for her.

Falling back onto the fluff of the pillow framed by her feathered hair, she was the picture of elegance. Then he saw it. On her chest. It was not cream, nor could it be perspiration. Something had dried on her flesh leaving a glistening print. Drawn in closer by his curiosity, he carefully spread the collar of her dressing gown wide to pull the neckline lower to investigate. His fingers brushed her warm skin, and he was ignited with a charge that surged from her own body. Her breast caught the dim light, and his gut tightened as he fought for a breath. They were round and delicious, waiting for his touch. Her skin was slightly puckered around the sheen of fresh wax over her bare breasts.

"What were you up to?" he chuckled.

Looking closer, he finally saw the droplets of wax that had burned into her nightclothes.

Aroused with a force that slammed his erection against his trousers, he was revitalized. Dressed in this erotic scene, Cynthia slumbered in peace, painting for him the erotic desires that have tortured him. Night after night, he had been punishing himself for wanting her while she had been satisfying her own needs with a flame?!

...No? It was not possible? Such a ridiculous thought had to be cast out. This was his virgin bride? His innocent harp playing Virgin who dressed in white chiffon... and crimson... framed with dark, sultry locks flowing down her back?

NO! This was not possible. Looking down at the side table were, the remains of a candle and a fingerprint imbedded in the wax under the charred wick.

He would have his answers tomorrow night, and if he discovered that his sweet pure wife had been holding out on him, heaven help the chit! After a month of fighting off his natural hunger, he was a desperate man with little self-control left. Her claim to innocence was the only thing keeping him from taking her now. Tomorrow, he would know if his bride was still an innocent or a banshee

Leaving her chamber for his own, he quietly closed the connecting door and planned what the next day would bring for him and his marriage.

Chapter 2

A good night's sleep was not always the answer. Passing the day away in a haze, the house moved at its well-trained routine as Cynthia watched as a bystander. Never quite knowing her mind, she had mixed up the menus for the dinner she and her Duke were hosting later in the week. She was calling her lady's Maid by the wrong name and ordered the gardener to prune the annuals forgetting what month it was.

It was luck that with every stumble she made, her husband had been there to set her straight.

When the wrong blossoms had been ordered for the foyer, the Duke simply smiled and told her how it was her ability for originality that made her so accomplished. Then there were the grocer accounts. The Duke's man of business approached them as they were taking in their mid-day break to point out that the grocer had been over paid by nearly double. The Duke only chuckled and thanked his wife for reminding him about how he needed to set the standards of charity. Even his tea had been wrong. Anyone would think that no sugar, no cream would be easy enough to remember after a month of marriage, but he sat there and only complimented her hostess skills while drinking the very pale and overly sweeten tea.

What had become of her gruff and stern Duke? Where was the brute that she had fantasized over the last month? Here she had been praying for the chance of a kind word and loving endearment from him, and now that she was being spoiled to the brim, she did not know what to do with him?

Cynthia had not expected to find her husband awaiting her in the parlor prior to dinner. In the last month when he had joined her for their evening meal, he would not make an appearance until she was already seated. This night he was seated in front of a blazing fire, sipping an amber beverage. His hair hung over his face, distorting her view of his profile, but it was clear that he was deep in thought.

"Excuse me," she said backing out of the room, "I did not expect to find you in here." Turning her back to him, she started to pull the door shut behind her.

"Then why come to the parlor?" Frozen like a statue, his question stopped her exit.

"Pardon?" Slowly, she turned her head and looked at him over her shoulder.

"If you did not expect to find me in here, then why did you come to the parlor?" Slowly standing, he kept his eyes on the fire, pouring the contents of his glass over the hearth, giving the flames an excited jump. "It is customary for a wife to join her husband before their evening meal to enjoy a moment of relaxation and refreshment," he said turning to her, she swallowed back her breath looking over his half-dressed state, "...Is it not?"

The simple bow at his waist was not enough to distract Cynthia from his naked neck and open cuff of his shirtsleeves. Having discarded his formal neck cloth and waistcoat, he was a man in half dress. It was not necessary to question if that had been his first "refreshment" that he emptied over the fire. Eyes as wild as his hair, he was looking more like a beast ready to pounce rather than her formal and reserved Duke.

Rolling her shoulders back, she forced her nervousness behind her.

"And as you see, I am here in the Parlor awaiting the announcement as I have been every night since our wedding night. The question is more of why has my husband failed to make an appearance here in *OUR* parlor instead of that club of yours?" Chin high and shoulders rolled back, she turned her back on him and made her way out to the door again.

Pulling the door open, it quickly closed again, and she was pushed chest first into the carved wood.

"You failed to hear the part of '*The Wife joins her husband*'?" His body held her against the door, his heat burned through his clothes.

"...I... don't understand... I was..." Stammering for the words, her body shook under him, already his erection was pressing into her lower back, fighting to be free of his confining clothes.

His teeth bit her lower earlobe, silencing her to a shuddering groan. Soft and delicate, she was like a French delicacy. And she was his.

"If I was not in our..." he licked the rim of her ear "... parlor, than where should you have been?"

Cynthia was silent and shaking from the rising need in her. He was behaving like a barbarian, holding her to the door, and torturing her with questions, but she could not comprehend the words. His growing erection was hard into her back and her face hurt from being forced against the door... she had never felt more excited or wanton.

"Answer wife!" A dominant bite on the back of her neck left a period to his command.

"With... With..." licking her dry lips, she stammered for her words. "With you?"

One arm released her and wrapped around her waist, pulling her against him and his stiff member. His lips were soft and gentle on the back of her neck as he gave her the most tender and loving kiss she had ever had... and the first of the kind he had ever given her beyond the back of her hand.

"Very good." Hot breath on her neck raised the little hairs and tingled her skin. "Now, the next time I am in my Library waiting for my wife to attend to me before our evening meal, will you be there, or will you be hiding from me in this small and cold parlor?"

His question spoke of a new truth that she had not considered. Was all of this born from just a number of misunderstandings? And why did her heart race when he addressed her attending to her husband?

"Yes," she exhaled. His impassioned dominance had her too dizzy to think.

Pulled from the door, only to be spun around, her back was pushed up hard against the same door. Body to body, he leaned down to meet her curve for curve, erection to V. The thin muslin held less resistance to his hard rod.

"Now," his head followed his eyes looking her up and down, "If you do not mind, I am famished, and our dinner awaits."

Chapter 3

It took all his will power to hold back his need. She had melted under him from his first attempt of force. It was no wonder she had shied away from him in terror on their wedding night? He had taken the wrong approach and scared away his innocent bride when what she needed was the security of his dominance.

Fresh and willing, she would have been willing to surrender herself to him there against the door if he had insisted. She was ready and primed. even if she did not know it herself. She had been dressed similarly when he first saw her - all innocent and white, with a touch of Crimson sin, and her hair wildly loose down her back. There was wickedness in her crying out for his dominant hand, and this night, he would at last answer her call.

"Husband, you have forgotten yourself?" she corrected him, struggling from his grip,

"The dining room is to the east and you are heading to the study in the west."

Answered with only a sharp tug and a crooked grin, they advanced.

"My Lord?" She tried, and still nothing, "Debracey !"

Pushing the doors to the study open with his shoulder, he had to bite down on his upper lip to hold back his grin and ignore her protests. The stage was set with an intimate dinner placed for two before a strong fire and dozens of candles... Candles! Just thinking of what he had discovered the night before only increased the burn in his already hard cock.

It was the point of no return, and he had to face his fears head on. Could what he had seen in the parlor be brought on by her fear and stubbornness? Were last night's wax impression over her breasts dreamed up by his overwhelming desire for something more or simply an accident, if so then his future happiness could be shattered beyond repair. Rejection from his Duchess once again would be too much for him to recover. The moment he saw her with that damn instrument between her legs he had been consumed with a need that consumed his every thought, one only she who could satisfy. If after this night she still does not submit, then he was lost.

Pulling her across the threshold, she stumbled past him.

"My Lord... why so..."

"Hear me!" Gripping her shoulders tightly, he met her nose to nose. "I am not a Lord," he snarled, "You should know your husband's title."

"I'm sorry ... I... " releasing a frustrated breath, Cynthia reached for the only name she knew he would answer that he would add to his ever present anger towards her, "Debracey then..."

"My name is Charles," he growled between his clenched teeth, "I am the master of this house." One strong masculine hand ran the long column of her neck and soothed her like a household pet, "...And of YOU." Biting her lower lip, he claimed her as his mate, and she submitted with a sigh.

Leaning his head back, he watched her tongue pull her lower lip in, running her tongue back and forth over his teeth marks. She did not fear his desires, but rather seemed more intrigued by them. Could she be willing to become something that he had never found in any other woman, a lover, someone whom he might one day share his heart with as well as his body?

"We are now facing a choice; cross the safe bridge most traveled?..," Stroking the side of her face, he lightly brushed her cheek and followed the line of her jaw down until he cradled her soft face in his hand. "We could lock this room behind us and dine ten place settings apart. ending this night in our own chambers. Or…" Gripping her chin, he lifted her face to meet him eye to eye, "… take the plunge off the ledge with me and see where we go?" Releasing her chin, he forcefully grabbed her mound tightly over the layers of her gown and pulling her closer to him, "Which do you choose?"

Adding spice to his offer, Charles tangled his fingers in her gown, stroking her sensitive core through the thick layers of fabric. Blood rushed to her cheeks as her juices began to dampen her gown. Innocent to the world of desires, she could not hide her distress in what she was feeling. Already responding to his dominance, Charles promised to make their journey one she would never turn away from once he made her body hum.

"Please, I don't..." Her tongue darted out to dampen her lips, and he caught it between his teeth before it could escape behind her lips.

Biting and sucking, he soon had her lips locked to his commanding kiss. Possessing her lips, he raged war on her tongue. Powerful and dominant, he kissed her with such force that he could feel her start to sway in his arms, growing dizzy with lust. She was nearly ready for him.

Fear and excitement raged through her when the kiss ended too soon, and he was once again leaning over her with his eyes ablaze with an inferno of raging passion. Husband or not, he was still a man, and men -as her mother had warned her- had needs that controlled there every thought. She had never understood, until this moment, how controlling and frightening those needs could be... or how thrilling it could be to face them head on.

Tightening his grip on her sex, she was guided to the awaiting chaise lounge. Her legs shook with every step, and she feared swooning if he tightened his grip anymore. Violated and enslaved by this unknown need, she was lost to his commands.

"The time has come dear, sweet wife that you fulfill your wifely obligations to me." Turning the two of them around, the back of Cynthia's legs hit the lounge, and she was forced down to sit, tilting her head back to keep her entranced eyes on his. "You have been sorely lacking in your wifely duty, and I intend to correct that."

Lying back on her elbows, she tried to pull away from him, but was drowning in his command. There was no escaping the sexual pull she felt for him or the building need between her legs. She was wet and aching for his tight grip over her again.

"No more excuses. No more pains or sleepless nights. You are my wife, and by God, I will take what is mine."

Before she could sound out a cry, he fell over her. His mouth silenced her as his hand pulled and tore at her delicate gown. A beast she could not fight off, she melted to the pleasures of his hands. Delicate threads finally gave under the force of his grip, her naked breasts now broken free. There was no sadness for the loss, she no longer thought of her clothes or modesty, the fire in her belly was all consuming, and she had to find satisfaction.

"And what makes you think I am one to be taken!" Covering her own exposed, she forgot in that minute what it was she really wanted. "You say you have waited night after night in this study, but what about all the nights I was in my bed dressed, brushed, blushed and waiting?" Swallowing back the quiver in her voice, she tried to gain more courage. "Only once you came to me and never did you say a word beyond 'I hope you have been properly prepared?' I was waiting for the man who I watched dance with so many Deb's half the season. You were my Knight; I would hold my breath hoping that you would look my way. You were every young lady's fantasy come true, and then on our wedding day, I was the envy of them all, knowing that I would finally be that special lady you would dance the night away." Her tension softened a bit, and her lips played with the hint of a smile. "Marrying you was a dream come true; until our wedding breakfast, when that dream turned quickly to a nightmare."

Dropping his head in shame she could hear he rapped breaths slowly calm and grow steady.

"I told you I was sorry. It wasn't me, and I was ashamed for what had happened."

Crawling back from him, she pulled herself up against the back of the lounge. This was not the time for her to pity him, and this was not the apology she had expected. In a single toast, he had shattered her dream and made her the most pathetic story of the season.

"You have not earned my sympathy! Don't you dare play the victim in this. You broke my heart!" Trying to pull her torn gown over her naked flesh, "You announced to all our guests how you had been blessed, not only with a bride you never knew you would want, but a fortune to boot. Then after tossing back yet another glass of that swill you drink, you turned to my father and thanked him for being so generous for the high price he paid to buy his daughter a title."

"It was not I. I had been surprised to hear that morning that..."

"No! You don't get to defend yourself here!" For the first time in her life, she felt empowered and confident enough to defend herself and speak her mind. "You ruined my life! You humiliated me before everyone I had ever known! And you broke my heart! My father had told me that you had come to him to ask for my hand and never told me of your financial problems. I suddenly believed that all those times when I watched you dance from behind potted plants and columns, that you had actually known I was there, breathlessly watching you, and that perhaps all this time, it was a game you had played? Then, on what had started as the happiest day of my life, you shattered all of my dreams in that one cursed speech."

Silence.

"It was then that I realized, that only your uncle and a single friend represented you that day, and your friend's looks were not of admiration but repugnance. What I can't understand is, how could you hate me so much? How could you take such pride in my ruination, when I had just vowed to love and honor you with all my heart... and you had just done the same?"

Concerned with no manipulative feminine tears coming from her eyes, Charles saw she was on fire with anger... at him! This was not the quiet, passive, sweet, youngish thing he had married, this was the lustful, young woman he had seen playing the harp, breaking free of her white muslin. Remembering the waxy handprint on her chest the night before, he was finally seeing the woman he had hoped he married and not the shrinking miss who had quietly cried into her kerchief on their wedding day.

Why had he wasted so much time?

Why had he not seen that she was everything he had wanted?

Why had he forced himself to hate her for her father's treatment?

"You do not understand... what it was that your father had done to me.... I... I... I accepted your father's offer for your hand in marriage with the best intention." This confession was going to kill him if he did not stop choking on every word. She looked so angry that he began to fear what she would do to him. When would she finally strike? Her sex was always more brutal and cunning in their attack.

The weaker species. Ha! They knew what they were and of what they were capable. They knew how lethal they could be! But when would she finally pounce?

"And they paved the way to this hell." Her words stung.

"You must understand. I had already succumbed to the knowledge that I would never have a love match. My family's estates meant more than my single happiness. I was born with the knowledge that far too many depended on me... something a merchant's daughter could never understand. If the estates crumbled into bankruptcy, then so too would all the lands that my tenants have lived and worked for generations. My decisions were beyond me. That day, your father and my uncle made a point to remind me of that several times." Pushing himself off of her, he crossed to the fire, watching the flames fight for what little air his deep and nervous breaths left.

How much should he tell her? And how much could he tell her?

"That morning, you were a vision dressed in your white gown and bonnet, holding the bouquet of white roses and lilies that I had sent you that morning." The memories warmed, and he grew aroused, just as he had the first moment he saw her enter the church on her father's arm. "That crimson rose tucked under your thumbs. I had placed it in the center of the arrangement... a bold statement of the fire that I knew you hid inside." . Looking over his shoulder, his breath was taken away and his cock was hit hard with lust. Draped over the arm of the lounge, she held tattered pieces of her torn gown over her very exposed breasts. She was lush and ripe for him. If she could only see him the way he saw her, they would not be spending this night talking.

"I know there was much not said between us that day..."

"There was nothing! You never even tried to offer an introduction." There it was. The first tears pooled in her eyes. "From the moment my father had told me that you had asked for me...ME. I waited every day in our drawing room, dressed and ready to receive you. I knew that you would come, that is what gentlemen do when they have asked for a lady's hand, but you never came." There it went... one single tear rolled down her cheek and dripped finely from her top lip. "For a month I waited and I listened to every word of gossip, expecting to hear that you had been called away or were suffering from some grave accident, but no, there was nothing as noble as that. All I ever heard was of your regular visits to that bawdy house." The words were poison from her lips. "Even the night before you met me at the chapel you decided to make an appearance," and grumbling to herself. "One, I had hope was meant to be your last."

Wincing at the truthful stabs of her words, Charles realized he was close to losing all of this soon.

She spoke the truth, but there was so much she did not know. Yes, he had wronged her. He had never come to call and court her as he should. Just the image of her dressed everyday waiting for him as she had that day seated at her harp, pained him for his lack of conduct. He was shamed by his actions, but he was also hurt. There he was facing a lifetime imprisonment brought on by his uncle and her father the warden. The two of them gave him no choice in the matter, it was marriage to Cynthia or face financial ruin. He resented her despite what he had felt that first time he saw her. Yes, perhaps he had focused on the more lusty choices at the Balls during the season and never gave a glance to the wall, but what bachelor would give notice to all the chaperones and flowers that sat there waiting for their knight that would never come.

Fighting for the right defense none, could come out. He could tell her how he felt trapped, how he had seen her once, but his uncle refused for him to visit for fear he might botch the whole thing, or that he was a victim in all of this, shackled to a virgin... but his honor would not allow any of it out. In the end, he said the only thing that was right and honest.

"I'm sorry."

Chapter 4

Sorry? Sorry? Was his apology what she really wanted? He seemed sincere, but could he be trusted? His head dropping down in shame, he turned back to face the fire. Gripping the mantel with both fists, she watched his white-knuckle grip and took caution. He had never seemed like a brute to strike, but perhaps there was a limit that she could push?

"It is a start." Her eyes traveled down his back, over the curve of every muscle that the linen clung to. No doubt this is what her friend Viola had meant when she said, "a fine specimen". In shame she had spent so many nights watching him dance and imagining what it would be like to see all that he hid under his formal overcoat. Now she could see the seat in his pants pull tight over his firm round behind. Biting back a smile, she distracted herself from the painful memories of their tragic wedding day. So often, Bea had told her lustful tales that she had read in her sister's secret copy of *The Pearl*, and in all of the scenes, she visualized it was her Duke's face and body.

Now, after all this time and all of those dreams tossed out, here she was facing him - or rather his backside - exposed and served to him. She had to do something other than fight with him.

"This time, I have been properly prepared."

Never has so few words meant so much to him, nor had a voice ever filled him with lust like hers just did. Taking his own drunken words back at him, and serving them with her as the platter, left him cotton-mouthed and frozen for fear that he might climax from the sight of her alone.

Fighting his raging erection, he slowly turned his back to the fireplace and there, draped over the new, red lounge, was his beautiful wife. Her gown lay over her in tattered pieces, one arm propped behind her head, the other holding her bare breast. Her thumb slowly stroked the soft-top flesh of her lush breast... something that seemed so natural. She looked free with her sex and confidant in his sight. This was his dream come true!

"Are you not interested in ending this argument for now..." tilting her head, she raised one brow and playfully asked him. "...And make this marriage legal?"

These choice words were not what he had hoped to hear, but perhaps, it was the genetics she shared with her father that made her say just what her father had demanded of him that cursed wedding night.

As he took his first shaky step toward Paradise, her eyes betrayed her confidence, flashing her frightened innocence. Perhaps this was too quick for him to take her now as he had planned? But a wicked grin gave him the assurance he needed, reaching the lounge and his wife in only a few more steps.

Standing over her, he stroked his hard erection through the fabric of his pants. He was hard for her and he would make her understand what that meant.

"Have you ever seen a man's member when it is hot, ready, and needing?"

She gaped at him, her lips parted and ready, her eyes following every stroke his hand made. Taking her chin in his other hand, he lovingly caressed her face, her eyes met his and softened.

"I have no limitations to the boundless passions and pleasures that I will to share with you, but we have yet to find where, or if, your boundaries can be crossed? If anything scares you beyond torment, or you are unhappy and want me to stop, then say the word..." He paused for a second to think of the perfect safe word that would stop him cold. When the perfect solution came to mind, he gave her a wicked grin and leaned over her to kiss her nose. "... Say 'Harp.'"

"What?" pulling away from him, she was obviously confused by the innocent and unromantic choice of word?

"It is a word that is to stop me in my strokes. To simply say 'stop' or 'no' is not good enough since you might say both of them during our little... play." He spoke with gentleness that she had never seen in him before, but his hand never left the rock hard bulge. "'Harp' is a word that is not normal, and it is one instrument that could make me wilt with a single note."

Matching his eyes in defense, he knew what was to come.

"I'll have you know that I play the...'Harp.'"

"Yes, I know. In fact, I have heard you pluck away, and I must say, that you are one of the finest Deb's I have ever heard try to bring music out of that instrument."

Chuckling from her stunned face, he released her chin; running his fingers down her neck, over her exposed breast, to her hand that held and caressed herself. It was a happy sign to Charles that she did not resist his hold, but seemed eager to play once he placed her hand on the front of his trousers. Feeling her open palm over his confined cock, he released a groan that erupted from down low.

"May I see it?" her innocent voice was lush and seductive when paired with her question. Finding his strength, he reminded himself of character. This was perhaps his only chance to introduce his wife to what he knew deep down she craved and what he needed.

"Master."

"What?" Her puzzlement never ended, and he would bring her more.

"Or, My Duke,' if you prefer."

"That is not the proper greeting."

"And this is not your father's parlor or Algernon's." Another chuckle escaped his focused thoughts. To think of bringing this kind of play to one of the Queen's events would bring at least a chuckle from the sternest of men.

Taking her fingers to his lips, he kissed each one to every word he said.

"I (kiss) am (kiss) your (kiss) Master (Kiss) lady (kiss). And you address me as such when we are locked in our passionate play." Licking her palm slowly and suggestively, "Am I clear Cynthia?"

Pulling her hand away, she turned it over and back, studying her hand as if it had made it through fire without a burn. This was all more than she had been prepared for, but Cynthia knew that only in his hands did she find the strength she needed to meet him and his seduction head on. She just thought of herself as the wax last night, and he was the flame. He would ignite her passions and lust, and she would melt ready to be rubbed and eventually broken.

"I thought you only just recently asked me to call you by your name and to avoid using a title?" She tested him. He gave a calming breath before bending down to her ear and taking a quick bite before answering her.

"Master?" he corrected her with a smile.

Blinking back her fright she smiled back innocently.

"Master, you contradict yourself?"

He groaned in frustration and knew that she was testing the waters to see how far he would let her swim out before he snared her. "True, but I don't expect you to take my cock between those beautiful lips or let me spank that perfect round rump of yours in the drawing room before guests? Nor would I expect polite conversation when we are alone while I am pulling you along with a tight grip of your pussy?" She blinked in shock to his crudeness and to the growing wetness between her thighs.

"Master? May I see your Cock?" She knew that her words more than shocked him, they seduced him. He was easy to read when he was in need, and she was more than ready to succumb to his needs.

Taking her hand in his, he used her fingers like a puppet as he slowly, sprung free from his trousers. She did not give him a chance to instruct her, she knew enough tales from her secret readings of *The Pearl* to know what a fallen woman did when presented with a wanting man's piece... and her husband was an exceptional example. Licking the bead of moisture that glistened at the tip, she contemplated the salty substance before delving in. There was no trained technique, so it was just an attempt at a feast.

"My dear," his voice staggered, he had lost control of the situation, and she loved it. "Cynthia," her name on his lips was always a pleasure, but she was not ready to surrender. "My Wife... you must stop or else we will be done before we have... begun." Cradling her chin in the palm of his hand, he gently pulled himself free of her giving mouth with a "pop".

"You don't know how to play fair," he teased her, "And you need to learn how to listen to instructions." Tipping his head and raising his brow, she knew what he waited for, and this once, she would not fight him.

"Yes, master".

Chapter 5

Her words were a gift that warmed his heart. So much was said in two words, all the pain and hurt that he had inflicted stood a chance to be healed. In two simple words, she told him that she trusted him, and in that trust, he hoped he could one day earn her love.

This was not any common seduction that he would add to his list, this was the woman that, in the last month, he had grown to admire, desire, and yes... even love. Taking her hands in his, he gave a gentle but commanding pull, guiding her like reigns.

"Stand, Cynthia. I must prepare you." His instructions imprinted a puzzle on her brow, and he recalled what she had said only moments ago to bring them back to this, "You are now prepared up here" Tapping her temple with his free hand, he dove into her eyes. "...But now..." trailing his fingers down, he caressed the column of her neck, cupped one breast, and grazed a nipple with the pad of his thumb -making her jump. He ran the flat of his hand over her belly, until at last his fingers glided between the fold of her sex. "You must be prepared here." Gliding one finger in to the first knuckle, he pulled her to stand slowly.

Her eyes rolled back with the sudden jolt of pleasure that rushed through her. His strength and dominance enveloped her like a warm blanket, and she followed willingly.

Sitting down on the lounge, he faced his bride and pulled her to him. Her natural perfume filled his senses, and he salivated for a taste. Gripping what remained of her tattered gown, he freed her of the confinement in one strong pull, ripping the delicate fabric right down the middle. Shielding her body from the exposure, Cynthia was stopped with three simple words.

"Let it fall," he instructed, and she followed, releasing her breasts long enough to let her pretty gown fall from her, only to cover herself again. She was completely bare under her gown not a stitch to bar his view of the dark triangle at the junction of her thighs. Never had he imagined his innocent bride to be so bold. How long had his hidden temptress been concealing so much... or rather so little?

"Why do you hide yourself from me? A husband should see his wife in all her beauty." Pulling her hands down, he kissed each palm before releasing them and replacing them with his own. "You are womanly perfection." Leaning forward, he first kissed the underside of one breast and then the other, while his thumbs stroked her growing nipples.

Shaking her head, despite her boldness this night, she was still restricted to womanly insecurities.

Pinching her chin, he pulled her face down to meet him eye to eye.

"You are everything a man would dream of. Everything I could ask for." His confession was carried on a shaky voice, but with a loving, sincere heart. Kissing her once more, he kept his eyes on her. "My fantasy…" he said, pausing to close his eyes, he took in a long whiff. She smelled of sex and rosewater, "… My desire." Tenderly his finger sought the reward that had been denied him for so long. Dripping wet, he knew from one knuckle deep that she was his as much as he was hers.

This night was a chance for the celebration that they should have had a month ago. Then, she was shied away from him during their wedding breakfast, and she never came back. Perhaps drinking himself into a stupor was not the best choice, and perhaps he owed her a humble apology? If only her father had not demanded that he keep their wedding chamber sheets for his inspection the next morning. He had already completed his side of the bargain and was ready to find some joys in his new life, but his father in-law had to question his honor and insist that he provide proof that his bride would truly become his wife that night. Only it never happened, and in the end, he left his bedchamber the next day with a bandaged hand and a bloodied sheet.

That night she was a virgin, and she had deserved to be worshiped.

Pinching the sensitive pearl, her head was thrown back in her cry. Her quim surrendered instantly to his touch, sending electric vibes racing from head to toe. It was a whole new world invading her senses, and she was a willing victim.

"Come for me, my love." His voice warmed her, but not a word could she comprehend while his fingers ... and... mouth invaded her most intimate place.

"Oh, my dear lord," she mumbled.

"Come for me," again he instructed as his tongue plundered her Venus mound. She was warm and dripping wet for him.

"I don't... " she wetted her dry lips. "...understand?"

Sucking in her tender sensitive lips into his mouth, he was dominating her one sensual inch at a time.

"Just let go. Close your eyes and ride the waves."

She was more puzzled now then she had been when he led her away from the dining room. Her legs began to shake, and she reached over his head to steady herself on the arm of the lounge. Her body was out of her control, and her moans were not of her. She was a wanton creature of her husband's making, and she loved it.

Pulling her down onto his lap, he smiled into her flushed face. His eyes had always left her weak, but now, seeing his wicked smile glisten with her juices, he was heart-stopping gorgeous.

He brought out of her a rutting animal, and she was hungry for more. Tempted by her own pleasures, he now licked from his own lips. She surrendered and leaned forward to draw her tongue over his chin and lips in a long, slow lick. He was unlike anything she had ever tasted before, the perfect combination of salty and sweet, but it was his perfume mixed with her own that had the hair on her very visible neck stand on end. His deep-throated groan played a smile on her lips, giving her a rush of power and eager for another taste.

"Master?"

Answered with a raised brow, she licked her lips for the courage to continue.

"Please..." she tried again.

Her head tipped with a firm tug of her hair, allowing her to meet him brow to brow.

"Yes?" Smooth and dark, his voice stole the thoughts from her head.

"I... need more." Struggling for words, she asked the one question that would be her undoing.

Leaning forward, he captured her earlobe between his teeth, building her desires.

"More?" he taunted her.

"Yes." Fighting against the pleasure that ran through her body, she tried in vain to find the strength she needed to resist his sinful mouth. Holding his face in her hands, she pulled him to her mouth and took possession of his lips. The kiss was a wrestle of lips and tongues, and in the end, it was her steel-built husband who pulled away breathless from her kiss.

"Yes what?" He asked, not recognizing his own weakened voice.

Closing her eyes, she drew her lips in. They tingled and burned from their kiss, and suddenly, she had to have MORE!

"Master, yes, I need more," she confessed, "More of you! I feel an agonizing emptiness down ... below, and I need you to fill me."

Her confession brought on a new fierceness, and his hips flexed under her, pushing his cock up, stroking her naked belly. He met her eye to eye and spoke with a gentle control.

"Do you trust me wholeheartedly? Can you surrender to me body and soul?" He sounded more like the devil than a husband trying to consummate his marriage.

"Yes." Closing her eyes, she took in his scent.

"And whatever it may be that I ask of you... you understand that it is out of love and trust that I act?" Answered with a nod, he pulled back a bit only to be quickly answered with:

"Yes," she took a steadying breath, "master."

Leaning forward, he drew one of her puckered nipples between his teeth. Fighting for breath, one of her arms quickly wrapped around his head, pulling him closer to her. His teething was torture. Her body now burned for more from him, but before she could beg of him, her legs were pulled tight around his waist. He stood and turned around to deposit her back on the lounge. Arms stretched over head, she writhed like a cat waiting for whatever was next.

Rubbing his hands over his face, he was desperate to bring blood flow back up to process a coherent thought. She was driving him mad! Did she know how sensual she was? Did she know how desperately he held onto the last of his self-control when she wantonly licked her honey from his lips? She was a natural bottom to his top, but with some tasty fight. Even with her quick response to his commands and his role as "Master," he was still fearful if she would turn away from him once he began the next step. And if she did, would he still be able to establish a more conventional marriage?

She was a seductress draped over the lounge and no longer the virgin sacrifice. If he didn't drive himself into her soon, he would die from longing.

"Close your eyes..." His voice was firm. Taking on his role, he was now her master, "... and keep both your hands above your head."

Discarding what was left of his clothes, he climbed on top of her smooth, ivory body. His cock was hard, dripping, and he could smell the honey from her cuny. Reaching over past her and over the back of the lounge, he pulled the length of crimson silk he had stolen from her wardrobe, Secured it to a hidden hook on the lounge and wrapped the ends around her wrists. Pulling and straining to the foreign restraint, her eyes flew open in time to be covered in black. It did not take long till she was blindfolded and restrained.

"What is the meaning of this? I demand that..."

Holding his hand over her mouth, he leaned over to one of her ears, his lips brushing the lobe with every word.

"Do you trust me wholeheartedly?" She did not cease her protest. "If you do not cease this rebellious behavior I will be forced to silence you another way." His warning did not miss a beat, and after her next pull from the ribbon, he climbed onto her chest, holding her arms down with his legs. Pulling his hand away from her mouth only long enough to force the glistening, throbbing head in, he silenced her. Choking and gagging from the first few inches he flinched when her jaw tightened and her teeth threatened harm. Gripping her jaw, he forced her teeth farther apart.

"This is a lesson you must complete before I can continue your education. I suggest, my little fire ball, that you try to suck rather than bite," He said, snapping his teeth together on the last word. Still struggling, he stopped moving and kept only a couple of inches in. "Relax and swallow me down." Keeping his voice firm, he was able to relax in his own skin now that he was back in his comfortable role of master. He could never find confidence in himself as a lovesick puppy, but as a top, he was nothing but confidence.

"Relax," he said a little more firm. There was no threat of anger; he had to make sure his subject was comfortable and trusting of him. Pulling the blindfold off, he forced her to look into his eyes as he relaxed her jaw once again in his grip. "Now, you will take me down, but if you struggle it will take all the longer." She stopped all movement and listened, blinked away the moisture in her eyes, and complied to his instructions. Her lips parted around his cock, her cheeks red with a rush of bashful blood, and her brown eyes full and rich. She was everyman's desire. "If you only knew how beautiful you are to me right now. Seeing my cock in your perfect mouth is almost more than I can bear."

His words worked magic. With a deep breath she slacked her jaw and received a bit more. Sliding him into heaven, she began to suck him in more, her tongue exploring the sensitive skin under the mushroom head. It wasn't long until he replaced the blindfold over her already serenely closed eyes. Slowly, he began to thrust his hips, taking him deep and deeper into paradise, and her mouth began to grow greedy.

Matching his thrusts, her head lifted off the lounge, and she closed her lips tighter: sucking him in, savoring him. She was hungry for her husband. Never had she imagined that such an act was possible, nor would she have thought that she would have gained so much from giving him all herself. He was hard as a rod, but soft like a petal. Rubbing her thighs tightly together, she tried to pinch off the ache, but there was no relief. The more he thrust his hard member into her mouth, the more she craved him down bellow. Her dripping nether lips were screaming for him.

"Enough!" he commanded and tried to pull free of her, but she could not release him just yet. The feel, the taste, the experience was intoxicating and something that she could not easily release from. "Please love..." he panted, "... You must stop. I will not let this night end so quickly or like this."

Awakened by his warning, Cynthia released him and instinctively tried to move her hands to the blindfold only to be stopped by the ribbons. Cutting and rubbing into her delicate skin, the silk held tight and shot a line of pain and excitement to her womb.

"Leave it my sweet. It is best to relax for now. Just breathe and try to enjoy this as best you can." Tensing from his warning, Cynthia began to recall what her mother had described to her as the sacrifice of her innocence. Never one to face pain head on -and even more skittish of the unknown- her thighs protectively clenched tight. "Shhhhh." he tried to sooth her, but it would not help.

Lifting off from her body, he freed her of his weight, and despite her fears, Cynthia missed the intimacy of feeling him skin to skin over her. After wishing and praying for so long to be warmed by her Duke's kisses only now to be fearful of surviving the night she had dreamed of for so long. Feather kisses were all he tempted her with now. Softly, tenderly, he kissed over her bare flesh; starting at the curve of her collar; down the sensitive flesh between her breasts; over her soft belly, until at last, her breath hitched in anticipation for him to once again kiss that sweet spot. Heating her swollen pearl with his breath, he focused instead on her fleshy thigh, kissing and sucking her flesh until she once again melted under his lips.

"How is it possible to feel so much... When you tease me and ignore my... the... my?" Stuttering for a word, she could hear humor in her husband's voice.

"Your Cuny?" he finished for her, "There is so much sensuality and pleasure I am going to teach you. A whole new world I am going to open for you, but first..." He pulled himself over her again, dragging his naked body over her own, "I must make you mine, and in so doing, offer myself to you."

Slowly he breached her virgin lips and met the delicate membrane.

Chapter 6

'My Virgin Bride.' he thought to himself, *'How could I have thought she would be anything else... and how could I let that fear keep me from her when all I want is her?'* Looping from start to finish to start again, his thoughts were tormenting him. Perhaps it was a cleansing of his conscience that he had to tell himself how, in the end, her gift of her innocence was not as important to him as her gift of marriage.

Her breath hitched, and he surged forward in one strong thrust.

Clenching tightly, her fingers left red crescents in her palms. Capturing her mouth with his, he silenced her cries; the ribbon stretched and groaned in pain. She pulled with all her strength against the restraints, arching her back, and bringing herself closer to him.

"Shhh," he tried to sooth her, "The pain will leave soon. I promise."

"You have so much experience at this?" she asked him through clenched teeth.

Perhaps it had not been his best choice of words at that very moment. How was he to tell her that not only was she not his first virgin, but that in one night, he had taken three willing maiden heads from three very willing friends who ended the night with red asses and well-loved cunts? Even he had to blush at the memories of that night, but he could say in all confidence, that the morning after, he had very willingly said goodbye to his old life. That morning he saw his bride to be. True, out of desperation he visited a house of sin, but there was no pleasure to be found there for him. He had gone in search of a good fuck, but could not be tempted when the woman who had captured his heart was sleeping in the room adjoined to his.

'I am lost,' he confessed to himself.

Slowly her walls loosened and she began to relax around him, he began a shallow rhythm that grew with her growing enthusiasm. Before long they rocked with each other. Their bodies were in sync, where one would go the other would follow without a word uttered. Faster and faster they moved, now in desperation, his thrusts were powerful and she widened more to receive him. Holding tightly to her thighs, Charles leaned back, lifting her up enough so that he could impale her with greater accuracy.

"Charles... Charles..." Hearing his name on her lips in a moment of passion drove him over the edge.

"Please more... Yes... Oh my sweet heaven... yes!" she cried out joining him.

One final thrust and the deed was done. They both cried out one final time as his seed filled her, sealing their union, and binding them together.

The firelight now revived, and a warm blanket was draped over the Duke and his Bride. The crimson ribbon hung free on the hook, and Charles held Cynthia close to him. She had been well loved over the past hour, and the exertion was beginning to take hold as her lashes begin to flutter and her lids close.

"I'm sorry," Charles confessed.

"My dear husband, I think we have established the fact that I have no objection to any of the activities you wish to try." A wicked smile fought away sleep a moment more.

"I'm sorry for our wedding day..." swallowing back his shame and the lump in his throat, he went on, "... and for our wedding night."

"Pardon?" She was awake now.

"I never meant to hurt you, and none of it was aimed at you. It was all your father's doing." Now, he was certain, that his was not the best time to bring up his mistakes, but he had to continue. "That morning, your father demanded proof from me that our marriage was consummated, and that he would send his footman to your chamber and retrieve the linen himself. He insisted that if his daughter was not made a true Duchess by dawn that our contract would be void and all funds that I had received from the marriage contract would be returned post-haste." Pulling his arm back, he felt the cold loss of her body heat even with the thick blanket, but he was ashamed for how he sounded in his confession.

"So then it was all for the money?" Soft and weak, her voice was a dagger aimed of his heart. "I convinced myself that even if this were you finding a bride to fill the gap of children for you, it would speak better than to say you needed my father's money?" Rolling onto her side, she hid from him and tucked her hands under her head. "At least then you would still be wedding me for something that I could physically provide for you, but as a requirement in an exchange so blunt, makes me nothing more than an unwanted dog getting passed from one owner to the other."

"But that's not it..." Sitting up, the blanket fell from his shoulder and hers, revealing the two of them down to their waists.

"At least I know what I am worth?" The tremble in her voice made her sound weaker and weaker.

Rolling her onto her back, he held her down. The lounge was narrow, and he had to climb on top of her to make room, something that perhaps brought on an unwanted reaction for she flinched in fright when his growing cock rubbed her belly.

"Please, you must understand. I fell in love with you the first moment I saw you, and it was not at the altar on our wedding day. Nor, I am sad to say, was it those secret glances at the Balls that you dreamed of. I first saw you the day I was told of our engagement."

"But you never came to call on..."

"I did. My Uncle and I came to your home to discuss the engagement with your father, and I managed to sneak away while they discussed the details. That was when I heard your blasted harp."

Clenching under him, he saw her face go tight, and he fought back a laugh. Leaning over Cynthia, he softly kissed the tip of her nose.

"I despise the Harp and Flute and Piano Forte and any other instrument every mother of the ton chooses that turn their daughters from charming pieces of lace to trained poodles on parade." Kissing her eyes one by one, he smiled into her face. "But despite my dislike for the blasted thing, I am thankful that you chose that time to practice. When I heard the plucking I knew it had to be my future wife practicing whatever mundane melody your mother or tutor had chosen for you to play at whatever musical event that, no doubt, I would be dragged to once the announcement was made. I decided that I had to take some control in this, so I decided that it was time I made my presence known to you. But when I looked in, I saw you seated by the window in your white dress with a crimson sash; you had no inhibitions holding your harp and exposed a bit of ankle from how you had pulled the instrument to you." With that, he slowly drove into her.

Clenching her lips around him, Cynthia gasped at the invasion. Charles knew that it was a gamble to take her in mid-confection, but with his wife he had little self-control.

"In that brief moment, I knew that you were not some brainless Deb dressed up and trained to snag a titled husband. I knew that you were a passionate woman who needed to be set free. True, your beauty helped raise my interest," again he thrust deep inside her, and she smiled at his double meaning. "Your hair was perhaps the first thing I saw of you and that kept me interested to view everything else." Wiggling his brow, his eyes dropped to her breasts and his confession paused long enough him to lick the crevice between them. "I fell in love with you that day and that day I was denied an introduction."

"What? I was never given the option. I was told you were out on business and could not be bothered to meet your future bride."

Resting on his elbows, his hands were free to curl her hair in his fingers. The locks were soft and smelled of lemon and lavender.

"It was my Uncle. When he came to retrieve me after discussing the marriage contract with your father, he denied me an introduction. He feared that I would spoil things and frighten you away. That day, I was packed up and sent away to the country like a twelve year old boy sent to his room and not a Duke of five and twenty." He felt ashamed for how he complied instead of giving her the courtship she had deserved. "I was not allowed to see you or even write, and in that short time, I consoled myself with the knowledge that soon you would be my wife and no one would keep me away from you again. Then you father came to see me that morning and reminded me of what was expected of me-as if I was some horse set out to stud-suddenly I feared why your father was so desperate to buy you a husband and that perhaps it was more than just the title, perhaps there was something else and someone else. "Shaking her head in protest, he stopped her before he could correct him, " I know now that there wasn't and something I have also learned, I don't care if there had been. That was your life before me and this is now our life. Whoever - if any- came before me no longer matter, because I am the man you wed and not them."

"But what of the women you have known since?" Her question hit its mark.

"I am ashamed that I did go to a house of sin, but you must understand what you have done to me. I have been tortured over wanting you and never getting to have even a taste. Night after night, I have gone to your room, only to watch you sleep; knowing all along that I was nothing more to you than a way to a title. The other night, I finally went to my old friend in hope to find some relief. You could never understand the pain a man feels when he is left in a permanent arousal for a month's time with not hope for release. So I went there, in hope for a one night visit to my past life, but nothing happened." He could see her disbelief. "Nothing Happened," he stressed. "Alone with a woman, I could think of nothing else but my bride, and how I wished it was her who was watching me with such lust and not the whore who was tied and ready for me. I could not perform; I could not even make an attempt. My body betrayed me and stayed loyal to you. So I came home to find you asleep in a chair. Taking you to bed, I swallowed my need and tucked you in before I took my own troubles in hand."

His slow thrusts began to take speed, again and her hips started to roll. She was a natural for lovemaking, and they were made for each other's pleasures.

"That night... that horrible night when I came to you, I had consumed more Brandy then I ever imagined possible. My heart was broken by your father's words, and suddenly I knew that no matter how much I love you, I was not going to be loved in return. I felt obliterated. I was a corpse left to rot, but a corpse still expected to act on command. So I came to you and tried to do what was expected."

Cynthia recalled the morning after their wedding night and the marked bed linen. She recalled the fear that her cycle had come early only to know quickly that it had not.

"But the linen, It was marked with blood even though we had not yet..." blushing at the wicked words that she could not say.

"Nothing more than a small cut in my palm that healed with in a fortnight."

"Of course, You couldn't risk my father acting on his threat."

"No I couldn't risk your father taking you from me." Wrapping his arms around her ,he held her tight to him. "You were mine and you will always be mine."

Taking him in with every slow and consuming thrust, she was riding on the waves of pleasure once again. Calling out each other's names together they collapsed in exhaustion. Running her fingers through his perspiration soaked hair, Cynthia smiled knowing that she may be his, but he would now forever be hers.

"I love you Cynthia. That is all that really matters. I love your heart and your soul, and if you were ever to leave me, I would wither away and die. You are my match... my other half...." She silenced him with a kiss

"I love you too." Her heart was bursting with happiness to at last confess to him what she had held inside for so long." You are the only man I have ever wanted and the only master I will ever yield to."

HER QUIET BARRON

London 1853

Saying that the women of London gossip would be an understatement, and to suggest that they do anything else over a pot of tea is completely ridiculous. There was nothing that the ladies of the ton would not discuss when offered the opportunity, and nowhere was better than the tearoom of Harrods London during the heart of the season. Here, every lady who was anybody came to discuss the prizes and jewels of the ball from the previous night. Weighing in their own opinions over the occasional scandalized couple who chose to take their vows; over the anvil at Gretna Green; over enjoying the lavish display of flowers; and over whose husband was scandalous with which light skirt. No one was safe from the gossips of the season.

Unarmed to the slings and arrows, Sophia sat rim-rod straight, holding her cup as steady, as possible. Distracted by the pains from Lady Fairchild's ball the previous night she hid her eyes from anyone who might misread her expression and prayed that by making a public appearance would put any talk to a freezing stop. A lavish wedding was only two slow moving weeks ahead of her, and Sophia was determined to make it to the alter untarnished.

"If you hold that porcelain any tighter you might snap it in two," Lady Cynthia warned her. Wed to the catch of the season two years prior, the new Duchess of Chentry was cousin and mentor to Sophia.

Stretching her neck, Lady Cynthia gave the tearoom a gander and caught only two set of eyes that diverted her own. No doubt word had spread, but it would all be for naught in two weeks. Raising a brow in their direction, she staked her social claim in protecting her cousin. Any lady eager for their daughter's successful launch would not risk a cut direct from the Duchess, and Cynthia gambled on her social standing to protect Sophia's name.

"I can't bear the thought that all of those old bats are looking at me thinking that my success of the season is a dirty shame." Looking up, Sophia gave her cousin the first glance of her red-rimed eyes. She had shamefully been hiding her tears to the world and would soon have to hide them behind a wedding veil. "Why do they have to even talk about it? It is not as though they even care about whether or not we are happy, so why do they waste their time with the gossip?" Looking down at her folded napkin, she tried to busy her hands.

"Enough of this," Lady Cynthia scolded, "Your man has flaws... Whose doesn't?" Dropping her napkin on the place setting, she leaned over the table, lowering her voice in hushed tones, "You had best learn now that no man is perfect, and not all Dukes, Earls and Lords are great husband material. Mine was not the ideal launch into marital bliss, but..."

Sophia jumped in her seat in shock unable to comprehend what she had just heard confessed.

"But you have the marriage of my dreams." Sophia eyes glazed over in a romantic euphoria. "I can think of no other man and woman more suited than the two of you."

Nodding her head, she silenced the young deb. There was much that lady Cynthia could tell young Sophia about the pains and labor it took to bring about a successful marriage, but she did not see the need to scare her. With the wedding a fortnight away, the best approach was to talk only of the benefits of marriage and perhaps this would be as good time as any to imply on the secret joys to marriage, that was now only a fortnight away.

"You best know now that we were not always so blissful, and even now it takes work on both our parts to keep our marriage alive, but nothing has ever given me more joy... or pleasure."

Bright, blue eyes looked up with intrigue.

"Ah, now I see that I have your attention." Lady Cynthia smiled at her cousin's interest. "You best know it now that not all husbands lean on their mistresses for the pleasures of the flesh. And mine is no exception."

Holding her napkin to shield her voice, Sophia leaned over the table.

"We are in public," she warned her, but Lady Cynthia took no head.

"And we are in a room of grown women, most of whom are mothers and whose marriages you would learn best what not to do." Looking to her right, she nodded her head to a table of haughty ladies who clucked and cackled. "No doubt they would teach you well of how to keep your future husband at arm's length with only the occasional coupling that leaves you clothed from the waist up. You best learn now Sophia, that men are not the only ones who can experience the pleasures of a marriage bed, and when you truly give yourself to your husband, a whole new world is opened up to you. I myself waited a month to learn this lesson."

"But you and Charles are the love story of my dreams." Sophia felt like she had just been told that fairies didn't exist.

"Not in the beginning. I will not bore you with details, but for this: be open to his teaching and be honest with how you feel."

The advice was not much different from what her mother had told her only a week ago, but Sophia knew that the source of honesty Lady Cynthia spoke of was a world apart from her mother's advice. The rules and conduct of the ton was complicated and at times unnecessary, but one truth was that a Lady wife was to breed and a mistress was saved for a husband's pleasure. Only Sophia wanted more of her life.

"I don't know?" Looking down in despair, her fingers returned to the needless task of folding and refolding her napkin. "At the start of the season I would have thought your advice was possible, but now... now that I know what is in his heart, or lack of, I cannot see much hope for me." Defeated in her confession, Sophia felt shamed.

Reaching across the table, Lady Cynthia held Sophia's hands still forcing her cousin to look up. Only a second passed, but there was understanding. Lady Cynthia had witnessed firsthand how Sir Ricardo Hastings Baronet had refused Sophia an escort in the gardens when lady Fairchild had suggested that the young couple enjoy the full moon. There were none who attended the ball that did not witness Sophia's shame, and Lady Cynthia knew that there had to be more to the young Baronet's choices.

"Nonsense. Your husband to be just needs some motivation." Arching her manicured brow, Cynthia's eyes burned with wicked intent. Suddenly, Sophia's aching heart was forgotten, and the two friends giggled and plotted the rest of the afternoon.

Damn!

There she was again. Spinning and twirling across the ballroom, Ricardo watched as his reserved and innocent bride to be danced, laughed and flirted with another eager youth of the ton. This one was an idiot, fresh from the nursery. Every giggle and smile that she flashed the newest dance partner, Ricardo counted the number of ways he would beat his jealousy out in the youth. At 25 they were perhaps not that far apart, but if he did pulled Sophia any closer, there was little chance of him surviving past pistols at dawn.

Shamed for his behavior the night before, Ricardo had sworn to show his betrothed proper and respectable attention, but she was never near enough for him to bestow them on her himself. Driving this night to the ball, Sophia had been playful, bright, and talkative. In the twenty minutes they had been locked away in his carriage, she had said more non-sense than she had during their entire courtship; in fact, nothing she did this night was in line with what he expected of her. Something was different, and for her own sake, it had best not be one of these popping jays.

There is it was again. Her bewitching laugh. The hairs rose up on the back of his neck, and Ricardo knew that she would be passing him once again in a dancing swirl. Never letting her warm bright smile fade, she watched him in the crowd as her partner guided her around again. In all these months, he had not seen her smile so since their first dance. What was it that had her so light on her feet? Who was it that she was truly smiling for?

"Quite a spirited girl you have there," his host, Lord Charles, interrupted Ricardo's thoughts.

"Pardon?" Trying to offer a smile to the unwanted intrusion, Ricardo casually plucked imaginary lint from his sleeve.

"Lady Sophia," gesturing toward the center of the room, Ricardo wanted to remind the Earl that he knew his own betrothed and that he could choke on whatever it was that he thought of her. Instead, Ricardo simply smiled at his old school chum.

"You need not fear for me, Charles. My Sophia will be a proper and loving wife." Even he didn't buy his own words. Ricardo hoped for only happiness, and before this night, he had no fears for their wedded life, but now seeing how Sophia had come alive with so many dance partners, he had begun to feel ripped apart.

At last, the music came to an end and his lady was escorted back to his side by her most recent dance partner. Looking down at Sophia's upturned face, he was warmed by her smile and caught a blond curl that escaped and fell over her shoulder. Soft and light, her hair was a golden treasure that he looked forward to see framing her face while her naked body lay under him. Ignoring the man's thanks and praise for the dance, Ricardo focused on Sophia's glistening cleavage and wondered how many other men had watched the abundance that she had put on display this night.

"Perhaps you might excuse us." He looked up long enough to ignore the young man's offered hand and bid good night to Charles. "I fear my bride to be is in need of some proper covering." Taking Sophia by the hand, he guided her across the room, passing curious faces and whispers.

"Sir Ricardo?" Pulling back from his tight grip, Sophia tried to fight against his hold on her, but under the needed cloak of dignity, she had to follow him or risk disgrace. "Where are you taking me?" she asked, but Ricardo was beyond conversation. Dance after dance, he had watched the men ogle what was his, and he would not stand by and watch any longer.

Retrieving their cloaks and hats, he guided his betrothed from the warm confines of the London ball and into the cold night. Not able to stand on ceremony or convention, he did not waste time in waiting for the driver to be alerted of his need to depart, and instead, marched Sophia down the row of cabs and carriages until he found the black, lacquer vehicle. Perched on the top with pipe lit, the driver coughed on a mouth full of smoke when he saw his employer charge for him with woman in tow.

"In!" he demanded, pulling the door open himself and guiding Sophia in with a shove.

Stunned by his brutal behavior, Sophia feared that her cousin's plan might have backfired. She had only wanted Ricardo to take notice of her and perhaps offer for her hand in a waltz or a turn in the garden. Now, dragged from the ball and forced into his carriage with no chaperone to look on, Sophia feared what the tattling hens would cluck about the next morning.

Holding her face in her hands, Sophia tried to steady her breath, but was shaken when the carriage rocked by Ricardo. Sitting across from her, he stretched his legs out and slipped under the hem of her gown.

"You look out of sorts." he asked sliding one foot on the floor until he found one of her ankles. Gasping from the foreign contact, Sophia pulled her foot away, but was instead shocked when he kicked up her skirt with his foot giving her future husband a quick view of what he would one day own.

"What has come over you?!" pushing her skirts down, "What has come over you?" Holding her disheveled cloak closed, Sophia was fearful of what he might do.

Leaning forward, resting his elbows on his legs, Ricardo looked like a predator eyeing his prey ready to pounce. Hot, shooting bolts of lightning shot up her leg when his large strong hand grabbed high on Sophia's thigh with a painful force. Never had her betrothed shown any sign of forceful or abusive intentions until now, and suddenly, her Baron was a dark, manly brute she had read about so often in her gothic novels.

"What has come over you?" The tension in his jaw could break trees. "You flirted your way across that ball room like a cat in heat." Gripping the delicate fabric, he pulled her to the edge of her seat: pulling her closer and closer to him, until their knees touched. The threads at her waist were straining under the pressure of his grip, heating her flesh even more.

"How dare you!" Slapping at his hand, Sophia was quickly discouraged that nothing she did would dishearten whatever his game was. Her heart raced so fast she feared that is would jump right out of her chest.

What was she to do? How was she to react? Her passive, silent, and distant Baron was acting like a... like a... like a man. Trying to pull her dress from his hand, he proved to be too strong and overpowering, taking both her hands in own of his.

"You saw no reason to defend yourself from the pawing hands of your dance partners, and you will not deny me the access you so freely gave." Pulling her hands out of his way, he let go of her gown long enough to take her by the waist and pull the huffing Sophia onto his lap.

She wiggled and kicked, but Ricardo did not move, nor did he advance. Holding her tight to him, he had kept a steel grip on her tight bodice praying that she would put an end to her wiggling, or else all of this would come to an early end.

"Enough!" he demanded, and Sophia froze in surprise. Never had he raised his voice to her, nor expressed anger. "You must trust that I will not violate you. However, you must also realize that I cannot allow my future Baroness to strut about a ballroom with every wide-eyed school boy eager for a chance to ogle your bosom up close."

Shocked and embarrassed, Sophia covered her exposed chest with both hands and regretted listening to her cousin that day. Men were unstable creatures driven by their most basic needs, and to toy with them was like toying with a mad dog. Choking on a few breaths that had been meant to calm her, Sophia pushed passed her upset and unsettled with the knowledge that soon this man would own her by marriage, and despite his brutal behavior, she still longed for him to give her the same exchange she saw in her cousin's marriage. Sophia knew what she had to do even though her pride tried to silence her.

"Ricardo..." Just saying his name was enough to make a woman go weak at the knees. "I never meant to bring harm to us tonight, nor did I intend to bring shame upon you by wearing a..." quickly she reached out for a word, but nothing came to mind when the carriage suddenly smelled of Ricardo and that was a scent that always lead her to distraction "... a... so..."

"A harlot's smock," He offered with the greatest intent to offend and was countered with her palm across his face.

The sting of his pride hurt more than his red cheek, and Ricardo grabbed both her hands in his again, holding her close.

"That is the one and the only one you may have," he threatened, "I will never raise my hand to a lady in anger, but you do push me woman."

"Let go of me," Sophia demanded in vein.

"I think not," he chuckled, pushing a smile into his red cheek.

The carriage rounded a corner and Ricardo slid on the seat, loosening his grip of Sophia who landed hard on her rear. Moaning in pain, Ricardo leaned down to help her up, but Sophia was bruised deep and would not give him the satisfaction.

"If you must know," she started, pulling herself up on the seat opposite of her mad betrothed, "This whole night was my cousins fault," she confessed and readied her defense.

"What blame can you pass onto the Duchess?" His doubt was not veiled, and judgment from his eyes stung Sophia's heart.

"No, I blame you." The pain went deeper than her pride, but Sophia refused to let this man see how deeply he had hurt her or how deeply she cared for him. "After the humiliation last night, I had to do something to keep the gossip hounds from tarnishing our marriage before it had even begun."

Confusion knotted Ricardo's brow. He looked at her as if she were mad and rambling.

"Last night, when it was suggested by our host that you take me into the garden for a quick stroll," heartache was quickly being replaced with rage. He did not flinch much less show the desire to apologize.

This man saw no fault in himself, nor his actions, and this enraged Sophia. Swinging for another attack, Sophia was startled to not only have her slap blocked, but to be dragged across the carriage again and pulled belly down across his knee. Kicking and screaming, she was silenced with a strong hand to her lower back and another across her mouth. Pulling with all her might, she could not budge his hand and began to hyperventilate through her nose.

"Shhhh," he cooed, no doubt with a wicked grin, but Sophia could not tell with her head turned down away from him, "My carriage is well known and by tomorrow, once word has spread that I escorted you home without a chaperone, it will not take long for witnesses to our carriage ride to surmise that you are the woman screaming and ranting like a mad woman alone with me." Pausing for a little chuckle before he leaned in close touching his cheek to hers, "I am only thinking of your precious reputation and the honor of our marriage," punctuating his warning with a warm kiss to her cheek. It was their first kiss since he first offered for her hand and the first time his touch wounded her.

He said the words like they were foul and vile. Pained and broken, Sophia wondered why he pursued their vows when he felt so vile toward their union. The realization that he was near disgust for her, crumbled Sophia's fight and left her limp to his abuse.

"What? No fight left? No bite or stinging words for your future husband?" He sounded almost disappointed at her defeat. "I had expected more of you, but it does not matter." Moving his hand over her lower back, he softly rubbed over the gentle curve of her back and over her round backside. Despite her petite build, she was curvy and soft under the layers of fabric, and for the first time, Ricardo was getting a full perusal of her womanly form.

Passing once more over her back and rump, his hand laid on a little heavier and left a burning trail through her gown. Over and over again, his hand continued in the same figure eight pattern, hypnotizing Sophia like a cat purring to its owners loving neck scratch. Only a cat never felt the same burning sensation that she now felt between her thighs.

To her shame, this was not the first time that Ricardo had brought on such a reaction to Sophia. From their first dance, she knew that this man had a dark power. His hold on her went deeper than the contract signed by her father, and she feared what he might do if he ever knew how she longed for a deeper, warmer, wicked touch.

Long, strong digits teased, petted, and kneaded her soft mounds, lifting Sophia out of the carriage and above the city of London. She was floating on a cloud aimed toward a rising plateau that was unknown to her. Closing her eyes, she focused on the sensations that were pulsing through her body like burning lava. Parting her lips, a moan tried to escape, but instead, she had the kissing warm touch of his fingers still clapped over her mouth. Closing her lips around one long finger, she wrapped her tongue around him and drew his warm finger in deeper, sucking and licking him.

"Oh, lord in heaven, you are a sinful treasure." Breathless and eager, he struggled to contain himself.

The cold air filled the carriage and ran up her legs when he began to pull her skirts to her waist with his one free hand. She missed his slow kneading strokes, but was soon treated to a new level of excitement. Just as his fingers pushed the linen of her drawers between her cheeks, Sophia felt the pressure of his hard, threatening erection pressing into her side.

Burning red was her face when Sophia thought of the shame in what she was willingly partaking in. The invasion of his hand was an erotic thrill, she would have cried out for more if speech were a possibility. The thin linen did little to shield her from his warmth, and had she been given her own pleasures, she would have demanded that he rip them away so that she could know the feeling of his flesh to hers.

'*You are a Lady'* she reprimanded to herself, but when did Sophia ever listen to anyone, including her own reason?

"You are a lady made for sin," Ricardo's voice was deep and panting.

And then it stopped. Just as quickly as he had uncovered her legs, Sophia's skirt was pulled down to restore decency. She reluctantly surrendered his finger from her longing mouth when he pulled it away and lifted her off his lap and onto the seat next to him.

"You think I am a brute," he told her. His dark, chocolate eyes struck Sophia with their intensity, "You think I do not see you and wish that I would pant and chase after you like those lap dogs who followed you around tonight. What you don't know is how I wanted to rip you from their arms tonight and claim you there on that very ball room floor."

Shaken by the confession, Sophia struggled to breath. He was dark and powerful, and she would willingly offer herself as a sacrifice.

"But last night... you... if you feel this way, why would you not..." She couldn't believe what he said. No gentleman confessed such a longing for his betrothed unless it was a love match, and their contract spoke of nothing but an exchange of funds- like a horse sale.

"Last night, I refused to be alone with you because I would not shame you." Locked jaw, he shook from the struggle to gain control of his own instincts and needs.

"Shamed?" she questioned. "But I am your betrothed. We are set to wed in a fortnight..."

"...And I will not allow those gossips you call ladies to question your innocence on our wedding day." Running a trembling hand through his hair, he took a steadying breath. The curls –a sample of his Italian heritage- wrapped around his fingers. "Last night, when I was offered the opportunity to take you to the garden, all I wanted was to take you in the garden. When I am with you, I can think of nothing more than how desperately I need you."

Over and over again, those three words played games in her head, fighting over their meaning and importance, until she wondered if he had actually said them or if the heated passionate exchange had just been a figment of her imagination. Looking to her right, he sat tense, but not completely out of sorts. If Ricardo had said another word, she did not know, and when he helped her down from the carriage, she cursed herself for that.

Standing on the street, Sophia looked up at the four-story grandeur that would soon be called home. Visiting Ricardo's town home before, Sophia knew the place well and was familiar with the staff, but she did not know why she had been brought there this night. Focusing intently on the front door as if this were all a figment of her imagination and it would vanish should she look away- she leaned to Ricardo and met the solid wall of his chest.

"I fear your driver has made an error." Her voice was an unintentional whisper. Sophia tried to find the strength to speak with more command, but something in this moment made her weak.

"My driver makes no mistakes and has followed my instructions perfectly," Ricardo corrected her. His Mediterranean heritage gave the command in his voice an extra, sultry taste. The son of a British Baronet and an Italian mother, he was raised with all the proper etiquette of a British noble, but glimpses of his Italian charm escaped from time to time. It was in those moments that Sophia fought hard to hide from him -and any other who might take notice- that she had fallen in love with the man who was to be her husband.

With a rigid back and extended arm, he offered her the front steps that led to the now open door. A bright glow highlighted the form of Adams the household butler. The poor man, who was the strictest model of propriety, stood ready for his master, but would not be expecting a chaperoned lady at this late hour.

"My dear," he gave her a gentle nudge in her center back and, Sophia took the instruction without fight.

"For someone so concerned about the propriety of our marriage, I am surprised you would risk a late night rendezvous." Her words did little in hitting their mark, and she was disappointed that she said nothing else as they climbed the stairs. He simply greeted Adams with a warm formality before sending him off for the night, insisting that he would attend to Sophia and wished to be left undisturbed.

With Ricardo close on her back, they climbed the stairs to the second level where she would soon find her room. The drapes had already been selected, cut, and hung and much of her personal items had already been unpacked. Sophia was familiar with her husband to-be's residence, and she feared she knew where he was directing her now.

The door to the master bedroom opened on well-oiled hinges and did not make a sound. Lit by firelight, the room had a menacing glow, but Ricardo made no move to light a lantern and closed the door securely behind him. She did not know what possessed her to follow him so willingly into this masculine den, nor did she fear what would, no doubt, be offered or enforced this night.

"For someone who fears the honor of our vows, as well as the reputations that we will be bringing with us before the altar, God and everyone else, I am surprised that you would bring me here."

Suddenly over taken by a chill, she crossed to the fire, never giving Ricardo a look back.

Sophia needed to find her bearings and decide what she would make of this night. No doubt she was now being offered a chance that she had fantasized about since the day he offered for her hand, but she just needed to decide what she would so with it? Would she ask for the one thing that she had been longing for during months of pointless balls and musicals, or would she demand her escort home and save this conversation for two week's time when propriety would dictate?

Holding her hands out to warm herself in front of the fire, she prayed for steadier nerves, but the orange glow only highlighted the shake in her fingers that she could not control. Stimulated from his attentions in the carriage ride, she could not look at him without looking down to that bulge he had pressed into her side. His manhood felt more like a weapon than a tool to beget children. Was it possible to have a marriage as her cousin speaks of? A love match with shared passion and love just as every girl dreams about? Looking deeper into the fire, she wished she could toss herself in rather than risk the words that were fighting for release.

"Do you have a mistress?" Cursing her lack of self-control and surrendering to the temptation, Sophia hoped that he had lost interest in her presence in his chamber and missed the question entirely, but his sputtered cough and need for strong spirits told her that he had heard every word clearly.

"I…um…I…" Choking on his words, Sophia knew that she had chased the moment away and was risking overstaying her welcome.

"Forgive me." Turning away from the fire, she caught one quick look at Ricardo who had discarded his coat and waistcoat and was standing in only his shirtsleeves and pants. Forcing her eyes to the ground, she kept her focus the floor to avoid the disapproving look in his face. "I should go."

Her kid slippers only scuffed two slow steps when a strong arm blocked her way and wrapped tightly over her chest grasping her shoulders. Peace was found in his arms, and Sophia didn't want to ever loose that feeling, but this was not her place yet, if ever. She hated herself for feeling so little and insignificant around the man she would soon call husband, but how could she believe that such a great man could truly want a woman like her.

"My silly, sweet Sophia," he pulled her into his chest and kissed the top of her head, "I will not apologize for my past, but..."

Two large masculine hands turned her around, and Sophia met him face to face. A smile played at his lips, but his eyes were pained and stressed. She feared the confession that was hidden in their depths and wished there was a way to take back her question and live in ignorant bliss.

"There are things in my past that I cannot take away nor would I want to." His voice was soothing, and he did not speak with the anger or resentment that she had feared. "Our actions in life shape us into the person we become, and I wish never to regret my actions. This is why I choose not to regret this night or the opportunity before me."

Her reply was stopped by his forceful lips. Their kisses had only ever been a formal exchange on the cheek or hand, but something had changed and he was possessing Sophia in an embrace that was quickly setting her belly on fire. Every kiss, lick, and suck he made, she matched until his tongue swiped across her teeth, demanding entrance which she unknowingly gave.

His invitation was erotic swiping inside her mouth, brushing the side of her tongue. Sophia surprised herself when she opened up completely to him and wrapped her own tongue around his: pulling him to her. By the tighter grip he had of her hair and clothes, she knew that Ricardo liked her reaction to him and she took one more, deep kiss before he pulled away from her and pushed himself a good four foot distance.

Pacing around the room, Ricardo ran his fingers through his black curls and looked more like a caged beast than a man ready for seduction. Sophia feared it was her and felt the similar effects of a bucket of cold water. Wrapping her arms around herself, she tried to find warmth, but her body still craved him. There was nothing she could do to take away the longing and abandonment he left behind.

"I'm sorry…" she started, but he would have none of it and put an end to her apology quickly.

"You have nothing to apologize for," he corrected her. "I am the one who has behaved abominably this night and should be beaten for my treatment toward you."

"Ricardo you mustn't," she protested, but again she stopped her with a wave of his hand.

Walking back to her in two long strides, he took her by the shoulders and pulled her close to review. His burning eyes and tense jaw were better suited for an animal. Sophia wished he would cast away the remainder of his clothes and show her how much like an animal he could be. Shamed for how she responded to his treatment in the carriage ,she was even more devastated to realize how she longed for him to force her hand again.

She was the shameful hussy who followed him up to his chambers alone and who now tried with all her might to keep her eyes from watching the growing girth pressing against the front of his evening dress pants. He confessed to her his shame in his treatment to her, but could she confess all the dark, wicked thoughts that were racing through her head? Raising one hand, she touched her side that had rubbed up against his member in the carriage and wondered how men could walk around with something so hard and protruding all day? Inexperienced and innocent, she wondered what it looked like, and even more, what it felt like unclothed.

Rolling his shoulders, Ricardo tilted his head and studied Sophia for a moment. Taking an appraisal of her womanly form, he gave an appreciative half-smile and raised one eyebrow at her ill fit in her bodice. Perhaps being ravaged in a carriage was not the best way to preserve one's appearance.

"You do not hold me at fault?" he asked.

"I willingly come to you and to our marriage bed," she offered and was answered with a confident smile that lit up his eyes.

"But it is not our marriage bed yet." Overly exaggerated, his expressions were playful and flirtatious. "Can you be trusted to not call a foul? Can I trust you to stand by my side as a wife and not run from the altar a fortnight from now: leaving me to stand in shame, alone at the altar?" Taking a confident step forward, his expression dropped into a sincere, warm smile. "And..." taking her hands in his, he lifted them to his lips and kissed each one longingly, "...can I trust you to stay at my side until the day I die?"

Her breath caught in her throat, and Sophia looked up into his warm eyes in amazement of the beauty in how he looked at her now. For the first time since he had asked for her hand, she could see the warm loving man she had dreamed of one day marrying. Nodding her head, she fought for her voice, but couldn't manage the strength.

"I...I..." She wetted her lips and released a nerve-strengthening breath, trying once more, "I will never leave your side. I promise"

He did not speak, but instead leaned forward and claimed her lips in the sweetest kiss either of them had ever known. His lips were warm and welcoming, and Sophia longed to melt into him. Few things in her life had ever left Sophia speechless, and this moment, Ricardo had managed just that.

"Then I ask that you trust me and in return. I will trust you to tell me when we have crossed the line of pleasure. After all, that is all I wish to give you." Leaning closer, he punctuated the key word once more: "Pleasure." Her nod would suffice in this hour, the sexual gale threatening to rage its attack on her.

He stood straight and tall, testosterone breathing out of every pore. Sophia's heart galloped in her chest leaving her light headed, but she knew the one thing she wanted better than she had ever known anything in her life. Watching intensely, she saw her distant, polite betrothed transform into the smoldering, sexual beast he had been threatening her with all night.

"Kneel," He commanded in a deep controlled voice. There was no threat, and before she could comprehend what he has asked of her, Sophia was on her knees, awaiting instruction. "Good, my dear," he praised her, but though his voice was warm, there was a new intensity in his eyes that made her tremble inside and out.

He cleared the remaining five steps to the center of the room where Sophia awaited him. Reaching down, he stretched his fingers over her head before dropping his finger tip on top, slowly running his fingers down until they were engulfed in the silky waves of her beautiful mane. His touch was soothing, and Sophia knew her reward was something to be treasured.

Pulling her head back, he smiled passionately down into her eyes.

"You are a good girl," he praised her, letting her hair fall from between his fingers, "Do you trust me?" His voice was soothing and all tension from earlier vanished, leaving this suave and reassuring Ricardo; The man she had always imagined she would marry.

"Yes," Was all she managed to say, and deep down, she knew it was all he had really required of her.

His smile stretched across his face, and Sophia knew that she had pleased him with her answer. The simplicity of a single word replayed at times can show the strongest offering of oneself, and in his pleasure of her reply, Sophia was rewarded with a warm glow that filled her belly.

She was his this night, and soon, for the rest of her life.

Reaching behind his head, he pulled the back of the white linen shirt over his head, revealing his perfectly sculpted body. Ricardo's skin had the golden bronze of his mother's Mediterranean heritage, highlighting every flex and pull of his well-defined muscles. Sophia was dry mouthed and breathless to touch him, and rising up on her knees, she tried to reach for him, only to be corrected by a firm, but not cruel voice.

"No. I did not give you permission to touch." Dropping the linen on the floor, he rested a hand on the waistband of his black pants. "Sit back on your legs and rest your hands on your knees."

She did not question or pause to think of the absurdity of his request. All Sophia could think of was she had to do what he said. Something deep within her saw the logic of this, and there was no question to that understanding.

"I require an offering?" he asked of her and was answered with Sophia's questioning brow. "Lean your head back," he instructed, "...But do not move your hands."

Dropping her head back as far as she could, she smiled when she felt the moment her long hair reached the back of her skirts. Her hair was long and silky, and Sophia's deepest vanity. As a little girl, she had developed the habit of reaching behind her and giving her hair a little reassuring tug when she was nervous, and now her mane was fanned out behind her while she awaited her first seduction.

"Gasp!"

Ricardo's hands reached into the top of her bodice and lifted her sensitive breast free. They felt heavy and round in her hands. He made her feel beautiful.

"This is the offering I require now," He told her. He used one hand to release the six, hidden buttons, allowing her to glimpse what every debutant had imagined, but denied to see.

Pushing against a chain, it looked more like a chained dog. The top was a rounded head with a straight base and appeared much like a mushroom. Under the rounded edge of the top was a gold ring that pierced the skin and was linked to a fine delicate chain that was tucked into his drawers. Sophia was disappointed to not be able to see more, but Ricardo fed her curiosity by stepping out of the remainder of his clothes, and revealing that the chain was linked to a leather strap secured to his right left. Looking at him now with only the leather buckled to his leg and the golden leash holding his rod in place, he looked much like what she had imagined a Spartan would have looked like before he donned his tunic for battle.

'Did it hurt?'
'What was the purpose?'
'Could he remove it?'

These were only some of the questions she could grasp out of the story that spun in her head, but before she could ask, he reached behind his rod to take a handful of the mass that was pushed back. It was so much to take in that she couldn't manage the strength to look away. Never had she imagined that the member of a man would look so threatening, and never would she have imagined that she would long to take it all in her hand just as he did in front of her.

"This is what you do to me," he confessed, releasing himself. Pointing to the gold leash, "As a gentlemen, I am required not to have such a reaction toward a lady... even my future wife, but with you... with you... I am like an adolescent boy." Taking the pierced gold ring between his fingers, he winced at the contact, but avoided as best he could touching anything else.

"I had this added on when I attended Eton as a boy who could not survive a day without embarrassing myself." Closing his eyes, he gave the ring a gentle pull that sent a shiver over his body. Sophia saw gooseflesh rise up in his skin and wondered, if a little tug of that ring could do so much to him, what would her hands -or sinfully worse- her mouth, be able to do. "I have not had to use this since those days until that first night I saw you at the opera. You were more than beautiful, you were a fantasy come to life, and from that moment on, I have been in pure torment fighting the over powering need to take you." Dropping his hands to his side, he looked intently into her eyes. "You think I have been cold and unfeeling, shaming you with my lack of interest, but in fact I have been protecting you from shame."

"Protecting me?" The words came out without her knowledge.

"I have been in constant need for you these past 6 months, and in that time, I have avoided being alone in your presence, not out of lack of interest, but because of my interest. I knew that if I was left alone with you, I would not have the strength to not shame you. Even last night, I avoided the Duke's Garden for fear of deflowering you there. This has been the only way I could keep myself at bay," gesturing toward the apparatus, "but now, in all your beauty, I can end this torment, but only if you know in your heart, that this is indeed what you wish?"

His questioning was beginning to frustrate Sophia. She was a woman fully grown and knew her own mind, why was it that no one could see that? Taking a deep breath, she assured him the best she could that there was nowhere else she wanted to be or with whom. He was her beginning and end. Ricardo was pleased with her answer and bent down to take both her hands in his. Her exposed breasts rubbed against her arm, and she could feel the fullness of them.

"Then take me away from my imprisonment and let me guide you into a new world." Lifting her hands to the gold ring, he helped her to find the small clip that attached the chain.

Trembling and cold despite the fire, she reached up to unclip the ring. It was small and delicate, but when the chain was released, his erection sprang free and rose up to his belly. Sophia couldn't resist the touch and ran her fingers over the smooth skin. It was hard yet soft all at once, and when her fingers reached the shadowed fold under the top, she was treated with Ricardo's gasp.

"Be cautious, my dear. I am a weak man at this late hour, and I do not wish to rush our time," he warned her, but Sophia did not take his warning to heart. Wrapped a hand around the base to hold it steady, she reach under to grab what he had been holding earlier. "Perhaps that should be saved for a less stimulating time," he said grabbing her hand away from his sack.

Dismissing the sting of his rejection, she leaned forward and gave into the temptation. His scent was salty and rich and made her mouth water. Extending her tongue, she licked just the tip, catching a pearly drop that had sprung free. It was slimy and salty, and she wanted more. He tasted much like he smelled and was something that she could only describe as male. Inserting her tongue through the ring, she pulled it into her mouth, and he followed suit. First, the mushroom tip that came in like a pop. Her mouth was stretched full. Sophia knew that from this night on, when someone made a reference to a full mouth, she would have a new image in mind. Pulling her tongue free of the ring, she circled and licked his erection as far her she could reach before the length became too much for her to take.

"Just swallow me down," he instructed her with a soothing voice, and in one swallow, she pulled him in deeper until he hit the back of her throat.

Feeling light headed from the rush of it all, Sophia was fighting for a way to control her breathing and savor the flavor, that was now and forevermore to be known as "Master" in her mind. She ignored the image of her mother's fright if they were discovered, and pushed away thoughts of everyone who would dare to stand between her and complete happiness. Perhaps this was not the conventional method, she defied anyone to try and bring her the level of pleasure she was experiencing now.

Running his fingers through her hair again, he took a generous amount in his hands and waited just a moment before he used her hair like a horse's reigns, pulling her to a halt. She released him with a pop of her lips, and Sophia looked up with big eyes. Looking for displeasure in his face, she tried to see what it was she had done wrong, but he answered her without the question being asked.

"You mustn't rush things, my dear." His half smile reassured Sophia. "This is not how I wish to finish this night."

Bending down, Ricardo lifted her into his arms, cradling her close as he turned to his bed. It was large, dark, and manly. The chamber itself was the perfect representation of him, decorated in dark tones, with clean lines, and simplicity.

"Your new chamber has been decorated and fitted for you, and will await you when our vows have been exchanged, but for this night, I will share with you my own bed." He laid her down on the turned down linen, and feeling the bedding give under her weight, she sank into clean comfort.

Firelight played in the room, dancing off the walls like a violent attack on the lovers' escape, and over Ricardo's naked body, it showed his perfection. Now that the chain had been released, and the leather straps removed from his thigh, she could see the natural rise of his member, and it looked threatening to her. Suddenly, Sophia feared if she would be able to fit something so large in her, and no doubt, he already knew her fears.

"You mustn't worry. It is a very natural need, and you will only feel discomfort this one time," he tried to assure her, but he had only added to her concern. "If there was a way to prevent you from feeling any pain, I would seek it out, but unfortunately there is no way around it."

Sitting her up, he began to unlace her gown and was soon lifting it over her head, depositing it on a nearby chair. Next came her undergarments, and soon she sat on his bed as bare as her breasts had already been. She was shivering from the exposure and tried to hold her knees to her chest, but met with a disapproving hand.

"You mustn't hide yourself from me," he scolded her. "Our bodies are gifts to each other, and you must present yourself to me with pride." She challenged his words with a long, drawn out appraisal that ended with the gold ring. "You still question this?" he asked, holding his erection in his hand and presenting the piercing for her.

"Does it hurt?" Reaching out, she carefully pinched the ring between two fingers.

"Only when it was first pierced, since then, I feel no pain there, and the stimulation is well worth the pain." A sparkle lit up his eyes when he said the word *stimulation* and Sophia wanted to know more.

"Stimulation?" she asked and released the ring.

Nudging her over, he sat down on the bed beside her. Goose flesh rose on her skin when his bare thigh brushed against hers and the realization that she was now touching him skin to skin. This was an erotic scene she had never read of or dreamed about. He was a figure beyond her fantasies.

"The ring gives my cock extra sensations and helps to tickle you inside."

"What is it called?" All of this was new to Sophia.

"There are many names for my member." Turning to the nightstand, he opened a drawer and pulled a small box out that he set on the stand. "I for one..." turning back to Sophia, he grinned with delight. "... Prefer the name Cock." The subtle drop in his open jaw was suggestive and made the word sound wicked.

"Your *Cock*?" She tested the words and blushed, "It sounds so wicked."

Taking her hand, he kissed her palm before placing it over his hard cock and guided her fingers to close around him. It was bold and sinful, and Sophia hoped that this night would never end. Under his direction, she glided her hand up and down his shaft. Quickly, there was another drop of the pearly substance that she had swallowed earlier. Taking her other finger, she wiped the tip and liked her finger clean. There was no time to savor his taste again, once her finger cleared her lips, Ricardo rolled on top of Sophia, forcing her down on the pillows and spreading her naked leg to offer him room. She was compliant, eager, and when their lips met, it was electric.

Naked and cradled between her thighs, every roll of flesh of his muscles was an erotic massage, punishing her with a growing need for him and only him. Lifting her legs up, she tried to open herself for him more, but was stopped with his hands. Looking up to him bewildered, he was a man in the raw: Hair disheveled, jaw locked tight, and shoulders tense.

"I am only human, and I do not wish to rush things." Gliding his hands down her thighs, over the back of her knee and calf, he caught her ankle and held it firmly. He stretched her leg up, marking the inside of her ankle with a kiss. His lips were soft and warm on her undiscovered leg and soothed the tensions that curled in her belly, but not the need. "There is so much I long to share with you during our life together, but allow me to show you this one treat."

Squinting his eyes, she saw a little demon hidden behind them. Turning back to her ankle, he began to apply a slow, erotic trail of kisses that worked down her leg and inner thigh. Sophia unknowingly began to roll her hips, stretching her leg up higher and opening herself all the more for him.

Lower and lower his kisses traveled, beyond where she ever knew a man would venture, until he placed a long, hot kiss over her woman's mound. He purred and cooed at her as one kiss turned quickly into three and four, followed by an exploratory long, slow lick. Shock took hold, and Sophia tried to sit up, kicking Ricardo in the head with her knee.

"I'm sorry," she panted and franticly tried to wiggle out from under him, but he wouldn't have it and held her still with a flat palm to her belly.

"Heel," he commanded in a soft and low voice.

There was no anger or harshness to him, just strength and despite the demeaning use of a horse command, she was warmed by it and put to ease by the comfort in his authority. Placing a hand behind her neck, he guided her back down on the pillows and placed, a salty kiss on her lips. For the first time, she tasted herself on his lips and was exhilarated from the aroma and taste of her sex on his tongue.

"Now, you must stay still and allow me to adorn you," he instructed with a softer tone. He was aroused beyond the ability to smile, but Sophia knew that, despite his harsh expression, she pleased him.

The click of small, tight hinges snapped followed by another snap of a small wooden box. Curiosity was driving Sophia crazy, but she did as she was told and kept still, waiting for whatever adornment he meant. With their wedding in two weeks' time, was it possible that he was about to present her with some precious family stone?

One tender kiss to her nether lips awoke Sophia from her dreaming, and she looked down just in time to catch his eyes with a concerned glint.

"This might hurt at first," he warned her.

"You have already warned me, so has my mother and aunt," Sophia encouraged him. "You needn't worry; I have already been prepared on what to expect my first time."

Nodding his head, a little chuckle escaped.

"I do not speak of our consummation." Raising a hand, he showed her a clip too small to be for her hair: and adorned with a set of three pearls and a bell that hung from one end.

Sitting up from between her legs, he held his strong cock in one hand. The gold ring sparkled in the firelight, and Sophia marveled how something could look so painful, yet so beautiful. Her fingers twitched to touch him one more time, but without his permission, she kept her hands at her sides, gripping the sheets tightly.

"Much like my piercing can offer us both pleasure, so will this serve a similar purpose." His instructions only confused her.

"How could that help to bring pleasure when it is meant to inflict pain?" Trying to take her eyes from his dripping member, Sophia realized she was lost.

He flicked the ring with his thumb and then let himself fall; he gave the sensitive nub above her lips a similar flick. Sophia jumped in surprise and tried to calm her heart from the electric shock of his demonstration. These lessons were going to kill her soon if he didn't offer her a way to find her release soon. Every nerve was alive and alert for his next administration, leaving her a quivering mess inside.

"It serves more than one purpose. Where it helps me retain some dignity around you in public, it can also find those delightful little spots hidden inside your folds." Taking his place between her legs once more, he used both hands to spread her lips apart and adorned her with kisses and licks that sent her flying off a cliff.

Over and over again, Sophia was rolling on a cloud of pleasure. With every lick and kiss, she was washed over with an uncontrolled wave of euphoria. Crying out for him, she lost all control of logic and thought and focused only on the perfect harmony that sang in her body.

"That's it my love," he kissed her one last time, "Let go and take my gift."

Snapping the clip over the top of her lips, Sophia jumped up to sit on the bed and screamed. Spinning in a whirlwind of pain and pleasure, she could not think or comprehend which was too much and which she couldn't let go of. Crying out for him once more, she was silenced by Ricardo's kiss and fell back onto the bed in his arms.

Naked limbs circled and clung to each other, holding the two lovers together and bringing them closer and closer, until Sophia could feel the first building pressure from his protruding head forcing its way in. The breach was slick from her juices, but narrow. She could feel her skin pull and stretch to receive him. The clip stung from the pull and push of his large member. Sophia tried to hold onto the pleasure that had drugged her only moments ago, but all she could think of was the uncomfortable pain of his penetration.

"Shhh," he tried to comfort her and tenderly kissed her forehead, "I am almost there, but I should warn you that your maidenhead will not give for me like the rest of you has and," pausing to release a breath, he looked longingly at her pink, swollen lips before kissing her again. There was so much tenderness and love in that kiss that Sophia did not fear what was to come as long as they were together. "I would not harm you for anything, only this is not to be avoided."

"Then take me." Taking his face in her hands, she lifted him to look her eye to eye and smiled at the wetness that built up behind his strength. "Make me yours."

Those words were the last of her innocent youth, he breached her wall and tore her maidenhead with a cry. The deed was done and nothing would ever make either of them regret it. Pausing for a moment, their breaths created a rhythm, falling into sync, and it did not take much longer till their bodies began to move in time with their breaths. In and out, their bodies rolled together, and Sophia could feel the three pearls from the clip rub and toy with all the undiscovered delightful tidbits hidden in her sex.

Wrapping his arms around her waist, he lifted her hips off the bed and took one of her breasts into her mouth, igniting a passionate cry from Sophia. Every penetrating roll led to another that ran deeper, stronger, and faster. It was not long till the two of them moved beyond the fear of the passing pain and welcomed the growing sensation that built up like a raging river trapped behind a damn. When at last their rising tension began to spring free, the two of them fell together over the edge and tumbled into a sexual oblivion: where no one else existed beyond the two of them.

Falling and falling, they held close to each other as if they were the only lifeline to find their way home once again. In an instant, nothing else existed. Nothing else mattered beyond the four walls that kept them safe from the outside world. This was what her life had been leading up to till this point, and she never wanted to go back.

Slowly, they both began to fall back to earth in each other's arms. Soft and weak, they held onto the other with a desperation that needed no explanation. Holding her close, he slowly ran his hand down between their bodies, feeling her skin pulse from the aftereffects of their lovemaking. And with a quick snap, he released the clip from her swollen lips. Sophia gasped at the sudden rush of blood and shuddered at the instant pain that quickly vanished, leaving her feeling naked without it.

"Thank you," he told her, breaking the silence.

"For what?"

"For agreeing to marry me two weeks from today, and that from this day on, to love me as much as I have loved you." Kissing her softly, tenderly, and without the fiery passion they had just shared, but with a purity that melted her heart. "I have loved you for far too long not to confess it now, and now that I have, I will never stay quiet." He kissed her again, and Sophia fought back the tears that were fighting to come forward.

"My dear, sweet, charming and ..." breaking a small smile at the corner of her mouth, she paused to look him intently in the face. "...quiet Baron." Punctuating her words with another kiss, she looked up into his eyes with a pure sweet smile. "You have had my heart the moment you first asked me to partner with you for the Waltz all those months ago. I give you myself, heart and soul, and I will never leave your side."

They met each other in a confirming kiss that sealed their confessions in their hearts, forcing out all fears of doubt, and chasing away whatever rumors that might had stung them recently. Fear and doubt could not come between these lovers again, and soon they would be joined forever more.

It was a bright sunny day when Lady Sophia met her Ricardo at the alter. Dressed in white and veiled from all, she walked eager and confident to meet her husband. Passing her family, and taking the last couple steps to take her husband's hand, a soft ringing floated from under her skirt unnoticed by everyone, but the groom. Her cheeks were stained in a blush when she saw the promising smile on Ricardo's handsome face.

Silence fell over the church as they readied to listen to the lovers confess their love for each other. This was the love match of every debutants dreams, and Ricardo was proud to take the woman before him as his wife and partner.

An Affair At The Opera

Chapter 1

London April 1852

"This is mad," Bea scolded herself. Turning away from the Theatre House, she hoped to make her escape before anyone took notice of her last minute flight. Her skirts were too full for even a well-trained dancer to maneuver in, and her corset was so tight that she feared it might cut her in two should she sneeze. This was, without a doubt, the silliest and most absurd idea she had ever come up with.

"Excuse me," she repeated to the unmoving crowd in the hallway. They were packed in like fish ready to ship with only one escape, but that seemed impossible for her to reach for the moment. Looking from side to side, she was getting panicked. Soon the bell would ring to announce the rising of the curtain and the fall of her reputation. When that time came, she needed to find her way free or march onward to her fate with no complaint.

"What do you think you are doing?" The voice was deep and the tone was much like what she had recently heard far too often. "It is too late for you to escape." Taking hold of her exposed arm, Max steered Bea through the crowd toward the awaiting box.

Pushing the red velvet curtains open, he pulled the wrap from her shoulders and tossed it aside. Missing the hook on the wall, and risking damage to the last of Bea's formal ensembles, it landed on the chair beside it. His whole demeanor was stern, and his jaw was clamped together fiercely. He was in a bad mood, and for the first time in over ten years, she feared he might draw blood this night.

"I never asked you to come," she tried to defend herself, "You only offered to see me safely to my escorts arm, but now, with your attitude, I fear you might have frightened him off."

"Lord Travertine scared off by a lout in a bad mood?" he chuckled. "I doubt that. You had best research your future clients better if you wish to make a success of this." Taking the seat beside her, Max stretched his feet out in front of him, claiming his right to be there. "He is a scoundrel and a brute, and his tastes are not to my liking, nor will they be to yours." Turning to her abruptly, he violently shook his finger in front of her face. "I guarantee that. You are better off dying in the street than to face one night alone with him. You know nothing of what he is known for, and trust me when I tell you that you want no part of it."

"You have no say in this matter, and you are starting to create a scene," she whispered through a plastered smile that did not reach the cold look in her eyes.

Looking across the theatre, she spotted her dearest friend Annabel. Together they had scandalized their coming out season with Lord Whimpslies wig in the punch bowl to their giggling shame. It was that same ball where Thomas had first taken notice of her and where Max had first managed to insult her company. Best friends since childhood, Sir. Edmond Maximus Dubershire the 3rd and her beloved Thomas had been inseparable when she first encountered the blood brothers all those years ago. Seated next to Annabel was her cousin Lord Charles Fairchild, or Connie as he preferred you call him, and beside him was the fresh face of his new bride Lady Elizabeth or Beth, as she had informally asked to be called. Both ladies had married up into society, but not Bea. She had married into money and with that came vast expense and sacrifice. A lady marrying into trade was looked down upon, and soon after her vows were made, she had been introduced to the cold reality of having some doors closed to her.

Regret was a word that Bea had vanished from her life the day she married Tom. She had loved him wholeheartedly, and with her friends and Max circling them, she had no need for anything else. Since the day Tom's ship was lost, he had been surrounded by her friends and comforted like family. Max, being her children's godfather, never missed the chance to take the boys for an outing and give them the needed time to create mischief as boys were meant to do. Turning to Max, she knew deep down that it had been his support and friendship that had kept her going, and if it weren't for her lack of funds, she would be home now sharing a night cap with Max before he bid her and the boys goodnight. If only things were different.

Time was rushing by, and the last few empty seats were being filled: still no sign of Lord Travertine. Had he been delayed? Had he fallen ill? Or worse, had he changed his mind? Too much depended on this liaison, and if he was not to be counted on, she would surly lose the house with in a year.

The pressure of this night was starting to choke Bea. She franticly pulled her hand free of her small purse strings-dropping it on the floor-and opened her fan to find some relief. Cologne and perfumes rose up from the main floor of the orchestra level to the private box. Vigorously, she tried to fan away all the sweet and strong smells while trying to cool her neck, but nothing was helping. The night was moving along without the appearance of her would-be benefactor.

The chandelier was rising up and the theatre began to dim, announcing the start of the Opera. With the first strings of the Orchestra ringing out, Bea thought she would faint. Reaching up to wipe her brow with a gloved hand, she was stopped by Max's hand grasping her wrist lightly. His fingers circled her wrist to hold it away from her face, but did not apply pressure when he opened her fingers one by one. Heat ran through each finger he touched. Bea dropped her fan from her other hand, letting it hang loose from the gold rope that was tied around her wrist. Open to him, he placed a folded white handkerchief in her palm

"You wouldn't want to damage your gloves," he whispered and Bea thanked him before wiping away the perspiration that was beading in her nervous state. When she reached over to return it to him he waved her off causally, watching the stage come to life. Reaching down to retrieve her purse, that had fallen she slipped the bit of linen inside and tried to not think about the results of tonight's failure.

"You are better for it," the dark hum of Max's voice whispered into her ear. Bea could feel his warm breath on her naked shoulder. His unusual blend of sandalwood and lavender swirled up into her senses, and Bea felt a little lightheaded.

"You know not what you say." Frustration in the moment help keep Bea's mind wandering back to the seductive heat running under her skin from having Max sit so close to her. Breaking her focus he leaned closer and placed a hand on her other shoulder, burning her flesh with his ungloved hand.

Praying that he would take his seat properly before Bea humiliated herself and succumbed to faint, she was denied her wish. Max flexed and stretched his fingers over her shoulder and kneaded her soft flesh. She could feel warm perspiration form between their joined skin and was overwhelmed with images she had suppressed as of late.

The fan did little help to cool off her rising temperature, but it helped to provide a distraction. Vigorously, she whipped it about, but no matter of batting could shake his hand from her shoulder. Either she removed his hand soon or Bea was going to fall hard in society this night.

"Please remove your hand from my shoulder, sir," she warned him through clenched teeth, but he only leaned in closer. Bea could feel her baby doll curls at the base of her neck brush his face.

"Why not leave your options open," he offered.

Looking over to the booth in front of theirs, Bea watched to see if her surprised gasp had caught the attention of two gossiping ninnies, but as luck would have it, they had their eyes on the Duke and

Duchess Debracey across the theatre house with the Duchess's cousin, Lady Sophia, and her exotic Betrothed seated side by side. Raising Scandal as the house lights dimmed the two young lovers shared a passionate kiss from their seats for all to see. Bea hoped that their physical display would take the focus way from her being accosted by her Husband's best friends for all the ton to see?

"You need to stop this at once," she demanded, but prayed he would not pull away just yet. There was something comforting to have him so near. "My reputation is delicate at best and you could ruin me if anyone was to see us now." Nervously licking her upper lip, Bea pulled it in between her teeth to bite down. The sensation only filled her with the desperate desire for Max to kiss her.

'Where was this coming from?' she asked herself, *'Is it wrong to suddenly desire Max so much and is it a betrayal to my dear sweet Thomas?'* but only a mad woman would answer herself. In the end, Bea had to settle with the fact that she was all alone this, but before she could say anything he was gone. Sitting upright in his seat, Bea felt cold and abandoned.

"You have no right," she whispered to him trying to keep her focus on the singers below and more upset at their distracting noise than appreciating the Opera.

"Pardon?" he made no move toward her, no doubt trying to give her a dignified space.

"You have no right to play with my emotions," she finally tossed at him.

"Play?" Turning toward her, Max grabbed a hold of Bea's shoulders and forcefully turned her to face him, "I play with you?" Every word was dotted with intent. "I have stood by your side all this time. Night after night, I have watched after you, Timothy, and Brutus, and when I offered to help provide you with what you needed to pay off Thomas' debts, you chose instead to sell your body to the first cad you could find."

His words rang true, but stung all the more. She knew that her choices were limited, and when Max had first offered to support her and the boys, there was a small part in Bea that lit up knowing how he wished to provide for them, but it did not take too much logic to come to realize that he acted out of the goodness of his friendship to Thomas. Perhaps it is wrong of her to turn to finding a protector, but how else was a woman in her predicament to provide for her children if not on her back?

"I don't need this form you!" she spat at him in a whisper, "You know as well as I that there is no other choice for me. I cannot continue to depend on your generosity, and the collectors are beating down my door. What do you expect me to do?"

"Let me take you to bed," he offered. The warm tone of his voice was an erotic stroke to her sex, giving Bea a quick shutter up her spine.

Every limb in her body froze the same instant: her mind did the same. She could not hear anything that was said after that, if there had been anything. Over and over again, his words rang in her head, and Bea fought hard against the warmth that those words brought to her. She was melting inside for him, and in those few words exchanged between them, her whole world turned upside down and sidewise until everything seemed to fall into place.

'Why couldn't he be my benefactor?' she asked herself and tried to ignore the logical arguments that rang in her head.

"Bea?" Max inquired, but there was no response. "Bea?" He leaned into her and still nothing. If she could not answer him when he spoke her name, how was he supposed to seduce her? Taking a cautioning look around, he saw no on one looking their way and decided it was safe to make his play. As a gambling man, he trusted his instincts and this was one feeling in his gut that he could not ignore.

"Forgive me, Thomas," he said under his breath before taking Bea's soft face in his hands and pulled her face to his for a heart stopping kiss.

Lips locked, they met in the perfect matching. At first, Max had to work Bea's lips awake, stroking them in nibbling kisses until at last she responded. Tossing caution to the wind, he closed his eyes and pulled her into him. Swiping his tongue over her teeth, she opened for him and met his tongue eagerly with her own. Melting into their kiss, it was harmonious until a gasp from a box behind them broke the spell, and Bea turned away from him.

Frustrated and aroused, he looked over his shoulder to see a poor young fool and the angry miss who sat beside him. Max knew how the young man felt, but selfishly, was relieved that they had not been discovered. A scorned reputation was not what he would wish upon Bea, no matter how much he desired her.

"You jump like a scared rabbit," he mocked her and smiled when her shoulder jumped up in defiance to his observation. "No one sees us. Nor do they care. Do you think we are the only potential lovers trying to take advantage of the dark theatre and romantic music?" Risking her anger, he placed a hand on her shoulder once again, and despite a quick intake of her breath, she did not chase him off. This was promising. "How could a man keep from wanting you?" Running slow circles, his fingers braved the border of her gown and ran along the edge. "You could bring almost any man to his knees with one simple word." Dipping a finger under the lace trim of her collar, he slowly ran his finger back and forth around her shoulder allowing him the slightest brush of one breast. Sensations of heat flashed over him, and Max feared what such an action could do to him. She was his best friend's widow after all, and he was condemning himself to rejection and guilt.

Shifting in her seat, Bea rolled her shoulders under his touch, but did not move away. Breasts rising and falling with every deep breath, he could feel the goose flesh under his hand and knew that he did affect her. But even if she responded to him this night, would it lead to his desired outcome, come the morning?

"Please," she whispered, and his heart stopped for hearing the longing that he had dreamed of. "Please," again she pleaded, and Max leaned in to try and claim her lips once more.

Turning her head out of his reach, Bea dodged his kiss and then turned back to him, showing Max her worried brow and red-rimmed eyes. "Please do not shame me," she pleaded, "I thought I was ready to shame myself this night for the highest bidder, but by the grace of God, I was spared. I know that soon I will lose everything, but at least I have been saved my dignity."

Her words hit their mark with a marksman's accuracy. Max was wounded from her plea. In just a few words, she shattered his hopes and dreams, forcing him to walk away from what he had hoped to be a promising future. How could he have thought that she would set aside the loss of Thomas and take him up on his offer? If only she had allowed him the chance to formally propose the arrangement to her, but he had been cut off before the subject could even be approached.

Dignified and proper, Max pulled himself upright in his chair, removing Bea from his reach. He would respect her wishes without question. Patting her hands that were now placed in her lap - clutching her collapsed fan- Max smiled down at her, and Bea's saddened eyes brightened a bit.

"You will never have anything to fear as long as I am near." Warmed by her trusting smile, he turned back to the stage and watched the remainder of the act.

Chapter 2

Applause rang out in the house, signaled by the red curtain coming down and the house lights coming up. Ladies wiped their damp eyes, and men stood to stretch their legs, eager to escape the boredom of the night. Next to Bea, Max did much as every gentleman attending did and stood on cue, bending to her ear.

"Can I retrieve you a refreshment?" he offered, "Some lemonade perhaps?" His gesture was sweet and Bea was anxious to collect her thoughts in peace, so she welcomed his offer with a smile and bid him on his way.

Once alone, Bea sat back in her seat, but noticed eyes passing her over. She felt exposed to all around. Rising from her seat, she chose to step out of view and take in some delicious snooping herself. Walking to the secure safety of the curtains that framed the box, she looked out across the seats. Several had taken their leave for refreshment and socializing, but the sweet and virtuous Lady Sophia was still seated, accompanied with her beau. They were set to wed within the week, and Bea couldn't have been more jealous. The fresh faces had a glow of love and a blossoming future ahead. She recalled feeling much the same at one time, but time changes everything.

Reaching into her purse, she withdrew the folded handkerchief that Max had offered her earlier. Wiping away a bit a moisture, she took notice of the elaborate B embroidered in one corner. Silver and blue thread made up the elegant letter, and a Celtic knot of blue and green weaved about like an elaborate snake. Rubbing her finger over it, she recalled ever stitch and could still the small stain under the top hem of the letter where she had pricked her finger with the needle.

"Where the devil did he..." Her cursing was stopped with the interruption of an intruder.

"Such language," the shadow corrected her before stepping in from the dark doorway and into the light.

Lord Travertine was just as handsome as she had recalled, but there was always an intimidation to him that left her heart a scattering mess. The cut off his coat was always perfection and never a hair out of place, but there was something else about him this night that she could not place: A look in his eyes that she had never seen before.

She suddenly felt disappointed and scared that she arrived after all and wished she had taken her chance to flee when it was presented.

"You do me great offense," he began with a broken smile that could chill a snake.

"Offense my lord? I fear I do not know what you are speaking of." Bea instinctively moved one step toward the door to the outer hallway and stopped trying not to draw her attention to her desired escape. "I had expected that tonight you would..."

"And I had expected many things as well this night." Taking a predatory step forward, he placed a hand on the wall beside her head and another at her waist, blocking her frame in and proving Bea to be helpless to this stronger man. "I was most displeased when you rejected my invitation to the theatre this night. I had hoped that you would have been sharing my box followed by many other delightful entertainments, your rejection was most hurtful."

He was mad and spoke in puzzles. Bea did not understand what he was speaking of and prayed that Max would return soon.

"My Lord, I do not know what you speak of. I did accept your invitation, but it was you who..." Horror struck her in the gut. His hand left her waist and wrapped tightly around her neck. Quickly, Bea felt all the breath in her body escape, and feared that with one quick squeeze, he would finish her off.

"Silence!" he snapped and lifted his hand, raising her onto the tips of her toes. "You are nothing more than another whore willing to lie and steal."

The stale smell of brandy and cigars made her eyes water. This was no gentleman, but a monster. He was the brute that Max had tried to warn her about, but in her stubbornness, Bea had refused to listen. Choking out a couple pleas for understanding, he answered her with a sharp bite to her lower lip. Her scream was cut off from the tight grip on her neck, and soon she could feel the metallic taste of blood dripping into her mouth.

"You are a wicked little thing." Taking a long lick of her chin he swiped away a trail of blood that had slowly fallen from her lip. "I am going to enjoy breaking you."

The tight hold around her neck began to ease a bit, but only tightened again when the sharp, agonizing pain stabbed at her right breast. He had managed to reach into the flimsy gown and was pinching her nipple between his fingers, it was puckered white from lack of blood. Bea tried to cry out in pain, but his tongue invaded her mouth and stopped whatever air supply managed to get past his fingers. She felt as though she was truly done for.

"Bastard!" came a growl from behind the wall that Lord Travertine had built in front of her. Quickly, his hands released her, as Max pulled him off her with the collar of his dress coat. Max spun him around to face the man long enough to take aim and lay a punch to his jaw, sending the man tumbling out of the door and into the hallway. Max took two strides toward the monster, but was stopped by Bea's hands pulling him back.

"No," she pleaded in hushed tones, "You have already done too much. Please let him go before anyone else sees."

Max turned to Bea and saw the terror in her eyes. Pale and shocked, she looked the victim and Max's blood boiled. He looked toward Lord Travertine who was regaining his feet and straightening his sleeves.

"I fear there has been a misunderstanding," Travertine tried to clarify, but Max kept his eyes on him, pulling Bea protectively behind him.

"For the Lady's sake, I will ignore what I have seen and suggest you return to you seat." Each syllable was dotted with his spitting hatred for the man.

Stopping himself mid-word, Lord Travertine chose to withdraw his complaint and turned form the box with a confidence that froze Bea's blood. It was only a couple of steps till he was out of their sight, but Max held Bea in place for a good minute before tuning her around, only to see the drying smear of blood under her very swollen lip. Max did not say a word to her or indicate what he saw. Instead, he turned back toward the door and after Travertine.

"No!" She grabbed at him and choked back her cry. They had truly caught the attention of many nearby patrons, including the gossiping sisters who sat in front of them. "Please. I beg you."

No other words had ever ripped at his heart more since hearing his best friend say, 'I am to marry the lovely Beatrice.' In all these years, Max had never imagined that he could be disarmed by this woman with only a handful of words, but it was the heart-wrenching plea behind her words that tore at him.

"If I must," he turned to her defeated, " I will wait until tomorrow before I approach him.

Looking over her shoulder, she watched heads turn her way and walked Max into the hallway instead, closing the door behind her.

"Why must you do anything? This is not your fight." Bea was not prepared to see anyone hurt in her name, and she still needed to ask for explanations to Travertine's obscure claims. "Let it just pass. What is this to you anyway?"

"What is this to me?" stunted and hurt, Max looked into her face with shock, "YOU! You are what brought me into this, and I cannot stand by after seeing how that man treated you… if I could even call him a man."

Wiping her lip and chin with the handkerchief he had given her, Bea was reminded of another pressing issue. The stolen linen was now smudged with blood and would probably never come clean. No harm done, seeing how she would perhaps never reach for this particular handkerchief again. Looking up at Max from the damaged handkerchief, she looked into the face of her oldest friend and wondered who was truly standing before her.

Wadding the handkerchief in a ball, she flung it into his face, which he annoyingly caught with one hand. Bea's breath stopped, watching Max's hand block his face with a confident defense. He showed the same masculine skill as he had when he laid Lord Travertine flat a moment ago. When had her friend transformed from the dependable Max - always there for her and the boys- to a two fisted rogue? And why did this new vision of him tighten her corset strings?

Through the drawn box curtains, Bea could hear the Orchestra play the opening notes for the start of Act Two. There was some relief in knowing that the music would drown out whatever they said her on. As long as she could keep her temper and her voice down within reason.

Smacking his handkerchief clutched hand out of her way; Bea leaned in, jabbing her finger into his chest.

"You are a cad and a lire. I am ashamed I ever thought I could be so gullible as to count on you." Her voice was low, but her words stabbed him with heart-stopping force.

Arms stretched out to his side, Max was lost for words. He could not fathom why the gratitude he had expected to receive was an attack on his person. Since they had been youths at her first season, he had never seen Bea display so much anger toward anyone.

"Bea what has come over you?" grabbing her arms and holding them down to her side, he put her assault to a temporary end. Wedged in his grip was the blood stained linen, but he took no notice of the handkerchief. Bea was seething with rage, twisting in his iron grip.

"You set me up! You said he was to meet me…" Her voice rose with every word.

"You need to calm down and be silent before I do something about this," he warned her, but she did not cease and swung her leg back to land a sharp kick to his shin.

Crying out from the sharp pain, he tightened his grip on her shoulders. Never losing his balance, despite the pain she had inflicted, Max released one of her shoulders long enough to stuff the handkerchief into her mouth and toss her over his shoulder. Bea's arms were trapped under her, keeping the linen trapped in her mouth. Frantically, she breathed through her nose.

"If you are going to act like a bedlam patient, than I will treat you like one," he cursed, carrying her down the hall and into an unlocked room.

Light filtering in from the hallway illuminated the small office with enough light for Max to see that they were in a converted storage room full of props, scenery and rope. He did not bother to look any deeper into the dim room, but grabbed the rope and dropped the squirming woman into chair. Holding her down with one knee, he made quick use of the rope and wrapped

her ruthlessly to the chair, but not taking the time
to tie her there. Holding the loose end of the rope,
Max closed the door and sealing them in darkness.

Chapter 3

It was a clear night and a bright moon shined into the room. Blinking once, twice, and three times, Max and Bea's eyes adjusted to the evening light and were able to make out each other's faces. Bea, still gagged with the handkerchief, was near hyperventilating through her nose and thought she would surely pass out before he released her. Luckily, that was not the case.

"Now. You need to calm down," he instructed, but she was shaking from her rage, "I will not let you go until I know that you will keep silent. Your reputation is already crumbling from what the gossips saw, and if they hear one more shrewish scream from you, it will be up in flames and there will be nothing that I can do to bring you back after that."

Letting out three log huffs, Bea sounded like a bull ready for a charge, but instead was able to steady her breathing a bit more. Max reached for her gag and gave a trusting nod to her before pulling it out. Smacking her lips, Bea's mouth was too dry to speak after the gag had drawn all the moisture from her mouth and was forced to listen for a moment longer.

"Now I know I am liable for an apology to you, and I humbly give it. You must understand that I never meant any of this in harm toward you, and I never intended to deceive you."

Bea's nostrils flared again, and she could feel the steady burn of her anger.

"I know I had said that I would help to arrange everything for your rendezvous' tonight, but when I agreed to meet with Travertine, I realized he was everything I had been told. That man is a monster, and I couldn't in good conscious let you leave on his arm tonight." Max's words were rushed and left him lightheaded. Images of his interview with the evil Lord flashed in his head, and he was feeling the same anger burn in his veins again.

Walking a few steps away, never letting go of the rope, Max turned in his place and reached for a nearby chair, but did not see the small dark object on the floor in front of it, stubbing his foot on when he stepped to move it. Bea gave a haughty huff at his pain, but Max coughed against the pain and moved the Louis the 16th stage reproduction to take a seat in front of her, putting them face to face.

"You do not know him Bea, and you do not know what he will do to you," he warned her, but it made no mark.

"I am a grown woman. I know my own mind, and I do not seek your council in this." Bea was not confident in her words, but she refused to see reason in what he said. "You had no right to mislead me."

"I confess that I was not a gentleman in all this. I apologize for my actions." Clearing his throat, he looked in her moonlit face and spoke from the depths of his heart. "I had no right to mislead you, on that I will not argue, but the end justifies the means. If you knew that man as others have, you would understand why I could not allow you to follow through with your plans. He is a monster who abuses his lovers. I know some who enjoy to partaking in a more active dominate love, and there is no shame in that, but what this man does goes beyond anything you could think of." His warning was sending a chill down her spine and reminding Bea of her still swollen lip.

"When lovers partake in games that can inflect pain, it is with a mutual consent and given so that they both will enjoy what the other has to give." His voice dropped, and he gave her a knowing look. "There is an exchange in trust that they share, guaranteeing each other's safety. Men like Travertine do not play by those rules. He is among a breed of monsters that enjoy inflicting pain, but never keeping the needed restraint that a man in his position should have. There are a couple of women I have heard of who were rushed from his bed a bleeding mess, and when I interviewed him in your honor, he did not waste my time in denying the claims, but rather took pride in them."

Bea's anger began to cool, and she watched her friend's brow pinch up in concern. Remembering the terrified feeling of being trapped in Lord Travertine's grip, she knew there was something off balance in his nature. However, with her arms trapped under several feet of rope, perhaps it wasn't Travertine who had the problem; perhaps it was Bea who had poor judgment in men.

"Jesus, Bea. Look at us? What are we doing?" Running a hand over his face, he tried to wake up his logic. "Whatever I might say, it is you who must determine the direction of your life. I know this, but I can't stand by and watch that ...that... monster, flay your skin like he has with other desperate women."

She didn't have to see him to know that Max loosening his collar and had disposed of his coat. Moonlight was a fickle thing, only illuminating what it chose, unlike the invading light of the sun. Over the lumps of furniture, boxes, and scenery, that the rays of moonlight ran over, a beam of silver light cut across her lap illuminating a few inches of rope and the hand that held it. Max sat safely in the dark, but she could feel his eyes on her.

"You warn me about how brutal Lord Travertine can be, yet you have tied me to a chair." Unwanted emotions were fighting to rise up from her throat, and she could feel the first of several tears flow. "You came with me tonight with the promise that you would see me safe when you handed me over to my new protector, and when you walk away, I learned that you not only had no intention of doing that, but you had never arranged for the rendezvous. You lied to me."

"I had to do something. You would have never survived what he had planned for you! He would have broken your heart and your spirit. He would have broken you! What if you were unable to escape him? I couldn't risk it." Emotions were clawing at his tone. "I couldn't risk your safety, and I will stand by my decision. You and the boys mean too much to me."

"Enough!" she shouted, but Bea knew she did not wish him to cease from his confessions.

He was the one she desired, and this night for the first time, she longed to hear him tell her the same. She wanted to believe that all those evenings spent reading her boys to sleep and sitting before the fire with her were out of a desirer in his heart and not out of his promise to Thomas to watch over her. She did not want to be a dependent or obligation. Her boys were meant for more than that.

The rope constricted her breathing more than her ties did, and suddenly, the confining feeling of not being able to move her arms was making it all more constricting. She had to get lose and she had to now. Twisting her arms, she tied to fight her away out, but no amount of wiggling would move the ties caught firmly under her breasts.

"This is ridiculous! You cannot leave me tied here like a…"

His lips silenced her protest. Screaming into his kiss, she fought against him, but Max would not relent. He had dropped to his knees in front of her and pulled her face to him, deepening the kiss, which she still tried to resist. Lips locked in a bruising effort against her stiff tight lips, but something in him would not allow him to surrender. Desperation had taken control of him, and in this moment of madness, he could not release Bea into a world where she was defenseless to a man like Travertine.

Pressing further, he leaned into Bea, forcing her legs apart to gain closer access. She was warm to the touch, and her breath had started to come in panting short gasps. Yards of satin wrinkled under Max's assault, but neither of them cared as he held her face firmly to his. Soon her muffled protests ceased and her lips relaxed, until at last, they opened welcoming his seduction.

In the madness of the moment, Max had dropped the rope. Bea's shoulders relaxed and she could feel the first wrap of the rope fall from her arms and land on her lap. The inch of flesh that the coarse rope had bound now felt exposed, naked, and soon, matched with another wrap. Bea's arms were free at the elbow and she took advantage, lifting her hands to grasp his shirtsleeves to pull him closer.

Despite the binding of her upper arms, Bea's breasts peaked out between the wraps of coarse rope, giving her the pleasure of feeling his warm, clothed body press against her. The starched linen of his dress shirt crinkled under the pressure of their two bodies, and she could feel his heat burning through, only to match the rising heat emitted from her nether lips. She put an end to her protest, Bea began to melt into his kisses, and Max responded with eagerness.

Releasing her lips, he trailed his kisses along her jaw and down her neck. Bea whimpered in protest for the loss of his kiss, but soon rewarded with the pleasures of his strong lips kissing tenderly where her neck and shoulders met. He had found the sensitive sport above her collarbone that made her toes curl in delight. Licking along the base of her neck, Bea was tickled by wisps of his black hair when he stayed centered on her breasts. The roped created a barrier for him to take full pleasure of her cleavage, but the compromising gown allowed enough of her to escape that he did not waste the opportunity to take pleasure in her.

Bea could feel his frustration as he lowered his head to move past the rope, but she jumped as best she could when she felt his hot breath on her now naked breast. Pulling the neckline of her gown down and lifting her out from the top of her corset, he had exposed her to the cold air. Leaning her head back, she closed her eyes and surrendered to the pleasures of his kisses.

No words were spoken and no other communication was needed beyond the sensual exchange between their bodies. He leaned down to his side, and she could tell the moment he picked up the discarded rope, but Bea was thankful for the scratchy bonds. Tied up, and separated from her free will, she could surrender to Max with no feel of shame. Humbled by the bonds, she was separated from any respectability of her actions and preceded to receive his erotic attentions willingly.

He feasted on her breasts, kissing one of her puckered nipples, before catching it between his teeth and closing his lips over her areola. Gently grinding his teeth over her flesh, Bea's mouth fell open involuntarily, gasping for breaths as she licked, sucked, and bit her own lips. Her core spasm from his focused attack.

His mouth was a direct shot to her now weeping sex that distracted her from him lifting the hem of the skirts. He gave only a short, tentative swipe of his finger into her juices, and paused for a moment, timed only by the shallow breaths escaping them. When his fingers first impaled her dripping exposed sex, Max was not the gentle gentleman she had experienced in Thomas, but was instead fiercely claimed by three of Max's fingers. Bea's hips jumped up from her seat in surprise, but Max only pushed her back down with his free hand and did not lift his hold.

Vigorously pumping her with his fingers, he did not slow down a beat, even when he released her nipple to kiss the underside of her breasts, before moving to the other half of the pair. Her release was a rising scream that first ran through ever muscle of her body from toe to neck, until it finally found its way up and out through her perfect lips.

Falling from the high of her release, Bea was abandoned by Max, seeing only the moonlit glow of his back. Expanding and deflating, his back followed suit, his deep breaths calming himself from the maddening erection painfully, would not go down. Her body still hummed from the after effect of his talented hands, but her warm and passionate Max would not slack his own need. Instead, he walked across the moonlit room, running his fingers through his disheveled hair. Bea was taken for a shameful decline, seeing how he avoided her after giving to her so passionately.

"Max?" Clearing her throat, she tried again, "Max?" Dropping his hands to his side, he did not turn to face her, but instead flexed his large hands into white-knuckled fists. "You concern me when you stand so silent." Rolling his shoulders was the only response she was given. She tried to twist her way out of the loosened bonds, but there was no hope in making an escape. "Could you at least release me so that we might discuss this, face to face like civilized adults?" Still nothing. "Max..."

Turning on his heels, Max said not a word, nor did he raise his eyes from her bonds, risking even a quick glance at Bea's eyes. Silent and stern, he unwrapped the rope, and turned away from her misplaced neckline when she stood. Pulling and tugging, Bea tried her best to adjust herself and restore some dignity to her gown. The room was dark, but the cold air in the room told her that she was a bit more dignified.

"That is a bit better." Fluffing her skirts out with a couple reassuring sighs, "Now, about what just happened…"

"What became of your under things?" he asked with a growl.

"Pardon?" Bea was taken aback from the coldness in his voice.

Dropping the rope, Max took a couple steps toward her. Standing a full head above her, he looked down into her large brown eyes and Bea felt like a helpless rabbit about to be eaten by the wolf. Something had changed in the minute that had past, stealing the afterglow that she had hoped to share with him.

"You are bare beneath your gown. What happened to your under-things?" Bea wished she could hide in shame from him this moment, but instead she was frozen with fear. "You were a lady when you married my Thomas and now…" Grasping her shoulder with both his hands, he shook her, struggling to gain control of his anger. "You were prepared for him tonight? Admit it?"

Never had Bea regretted a decision more. She had taken to underground erotica to help prepare herself for this night and chose to follow the advice in what she read in the Oyster to help entice her benefactor. Never had Bea imagined that the night would turn so quickly on her.

"You judge what you could not possibly understand." Trying to pull herself from his grip, she learned quickly that he would not release her until he was ready.

"I never judged you until I realized you were going to dress as a whore for Travertine!" The word was a punch to her gut, and Bea snapped. Kicking at his shins, she fought her best, but he would not let loose his grip on her.

"How dear you judge me! I am facing ruin with my two boys to support. You knew that I was out of options, and you even offered to arrange this night." Her voice burned like magma, "You betrayed me! Why promise to arrange this night when you had no intention of having me see it through." Finally, the toe of her kid slipper made contact to his shin, releasing her from his stone cold grip. "He attacked me just now, demanding why I had chosen you! You! He didn't understand why I had declined his proposal, which surprised me when it was you who had suggested that I let you deliver my acceptance to the arrangement! Why? I thought you were my friend. I thought I could count on you, but now I don't know what to think."

He leaned on a desk piled high with boxes on top. Bea knew that she had caught him, and she stood there unsure of what she wanted from him this moment. The white linen of his shirt glowed in the light and reflected onto his face. Bea could make out the tension in his brow, which only increased her anger. Only she had the right to be angry at this moment.

"Bea, you don't know what kind of man he is. I could not leave you unprotected for him to do with as he pleased." Now, with her exposure to Lord Travertine's darker side, she now trusted his warnings. "Now, after what you have experienced, you cannot stand there and argue away at my reasons. He is a monster, and I couldn't risk losing you to him." His shoulders relaxed and fell forward. "I know it was wrong to deceive you, but I had no other choice. There was no reasoning with you. Your mind had been set, and you refused to turn back. I told you I would take care of you, but I was not what you wanted."

Fidgeting, she folded her hands in front of her and tried to calm her racing heart. Bea was a mess and couldn't let her feelings weaken her defense. Bending down, she picked up the discarded handkerchief and held it out to Max. At first glance, his shoulders tightened and his posture straightened. He knew what she was about to ask, and he was already on the defense. Things quickly took a turn from where she had hoped to be and was dreading what she felt she had to ask.

"What can you say about this?" Holding the linen square closer to him, he flinched away like it had been a burning match. "You willingly offered this to me tonight and as a gentleman, I demand you surrender a confession to me."

"You demand?" He spoke slowly, rounding his mouth to every syllable. There was almost a predatory threat in the way he spoke, and Bea feared she was demanding too much. "You demand?" he asked once more.

Grabbing the handkerchief from her hand, he waved it in Bea's face, taunting her. Bea tried to push his hand away, but he would not relent. She feared what he would confess when at last he chose to open up to her.

"You know perfectly well what this is and from when. I will not fatten up your ego with the story." Throwing the linen in her face, he turned from Bea to make his way to the door. She held her breath in the hurtful anticipation of his departure, but was delayed long enough for him to make a confession to the closed door. "That night at the ball, there was more than one suitor vying for your attention, but Thomas was the grand one. I could never stand in the way of what his heart truly desired." Taking a deep breath, he pulled the door open and let the warm gas light shine on him. "After this night, I am no longer in need of boyish tokens to remind myself of how innocent you once were." Stepping through the doorway, he closed the door sealing her in the cold room alone.

Holding the traitorous linen square in her hand, Bea pinched it with her fingers, feeling the soft worn fibers and recalling when it had held her romantic hopes. The memories were so vivid that she could almost hear the string quartet that had provided the ball with the needed lively music to help bring couples together. How was it that such a feeble piece of fabric could hold so much power over her at this moment?

It was Bea's first and only season giving her the blessed opportunity for an introduction to her beloved Thomas. For days prior to her first ball, Bea and Annabel had planned that they would pass along a favor to their pick of the season. Lacking the domestic gift of embroidery, Bea had struggled for two days on the monogram and suffered many pricks of her fingers.

Looking at the fresh bloodstains that had already begun to dry in a dark brown, she remembered the thrill that night when she had first been given an introduction to Thomas and Max. Thomas was tall, with honey-colored hair, and a bright smile. He had requested the dinner dance with her, and Bea had danced the prior dances in anticipation, sharing even a country-dance with Max who had managed to offend her only a few steps into the dance. When the Dinner dance had come, Bea reached into her sleeve to retrieve her favor so that she could tuck it into his jacket during the dance, unnoticed by him. It was all such a young romantic idea, but when the time came, her handkerchief was gone, never to surface again-until this night.

How had he come to have it in his possession?

Why did she feel so violated and betrayed?

Where had it been all these years?

Why did she feel so betrayed?

Why did he return it to her this night of all nights?

Why did she feel betrayed?

Bea suddenly felt all her anger wash away, seeing no logic in her reaction, and instead thought more over why she should respond so negatively toward him and how he came about to have it in his possession. Was it truly a betrayal?

Concerned, that perhaps the pain in her stomach was not the pain of betrayal, but was brought on more from shame from her treatment toward Max. In all the times since Thomas' death, he had been there for her to unload all the worries and concerns that weighed her down. Sunday's had become her sons favorite day of the week, when they would get to go on a new adventure with their

Uncle Max. Those days always ended with her sharing a nightcap with him in the library once the boys had kissed them both good night.

A revelation came of Bea that she must have been blind to have not seen before. In the last couple months, when she had begun to weigh her options and considering a protector, she already had one. More than a protector, Max was her friend and a good father figure to her boys. He would never hurt them, and he would honor the memory of their father. Above all else, what truly brought a moment of clarity, was the revelation that he was the only man she trusted and wanted to protect her, and if possible, for her to protect.

Tucking the handkerchief into the neckline of her gown, Bea rushed down the hall, hoping to find him before his carriage was called around. Her skirts and kid slippers slowed her down on the red carpet. She slid and tripped all the way to the grand staircase where she could see through the grand doors of the opera house what she had feared. She was too late. He had climbed into his carriage alone, not giving the theatre a last look back.

Lifting the front of her skirts, Bea charged down the grand staircase toward the cold spring night. The doorman was armed with the task of holding the door open, giving Bea a clean escape into the night. Trying franticly to wave down the carriage, she ran past the front of the theatre, but he did not stop his driver. The carriage was now around the corner and out of her sights. She was alone, and rightfully so, after chasing such a wonderful man away. Now, here she stood at the mouth of a dark ally: cold and alone.

"At last my sweet, we are alone." The hairs on the back of her neck stood on end when she heard his voice, and Bea nervously licked the dried blood over the teeth marks on her lip.

Bea could not speak or run, but was frozen still when he grabbed her with both hands and pulled her into the dark ally. Digging deep into her arms, Bea could feel her delicate skin give under him the pressure of his fingers. Tomorrow, she would be marked by his brutality with her skin painted in black and blue. She only hoped that when the sun rose she would live to hold her boys again in her arms.

Kicking and struggling to her best ability, she was mocked by his laughter. He lifted her off the ground, swinging her around, until her back made a hard contact with the brick wall of the theatre. Bea's vision spun, and there was a violent pain to the back of her head. Her exposed shoulders burned from the ripping pain of the rough brick wall when he threw her into it one more time. He had knocked the wind out of her and stunned the fight out of her, leaving Bea helpless to Lord Travertine,

The stale, rotting smell –she had quickly associated with Lord Travertine- penetrated her senses as he pressed himself up to her, pushing her skirts up. Poor Bea could not fathom what kind of danger she had been dancing with earlier, but now cursed herself for not heading Max's warnings. Sucking in a deep breath, she tried to pull her head back to scream with all her might, but was silenced by a blinding pain of a slap across her face.

"Consider this your first lesson," he growled, wrapping his fingers n an iron grip around her neck. "You can scream only when I permit it."

Tormented with flashing images of Thomas, her boys, and Max, Bea realized that she might never hold her boys one last time or confess to Max what she should have over a month ago, but was too blind to know herself. Fighting for air, her head grew dizzy, and everything spun out of control.

Travertine's hand released his hold of her neck, dropping Bea to the ground where she coughed and hacked for air. She couldn't see in the darkness, but there was a shuffling of feet and another man's voice. His voice. Like out of a dream she had conjured.

"Bastard!" Max shouted, pulling Travertine off of Bea and pushing him to the other side of the ally. He watched the man stumbled a few steps before he gained his footing and charged for Max.

Catching Max at his waist, Travertine lifted him with his shoulder, pushing him into the wall just a few feet from where Bea had fallen The villain took a few low jabs, but Max had an elevated attack and brought both hands down onto Travertine's back with full force, crumbling to his knees. Max tried to move out of the man's reach, but was caught by one foot and pulled down to the ground. The weak sound of Bea calling out to him distracted Max from noticing Travertine standing over him. One, two, three kicks to his stomach, Max rolled over in pain, spitting out the brandy he had swallowed after boarding his carriage.

"You think you can come between me and my new whore." Travertine threatened. "One thing you should know about me; I am not a sharing man."

When Travertine went for a fourth kick, Max was ready and grabbed a hold of his leg with one arm, punching the backside of the man's knee with the other. A horrific snap echoed in the alley and Travertine collapsed in pain. He was disarmed by the agony of Max's defense and could do nothing but spit out curses as Max lifted Bea into him arms, carrying her out of the alley, and into the light of the street lamps.

Allowing his driver to open the carriage door, Max lifted her in and held her close. Her dress was torn in several places and she had lost one of her slippers. Max could see the red blotches on her face begin to swell and already take on a darker hue. Tomorrow she would be bruised and shaken, but at least she would be safe.

"Where..." She struggled for air and her voice was almost too weak to hear, but Max soothed her, combing his fingers over her messed hair. "... Where... Safe?" was what she had finally chosen to settle for. Her head was tucked under his chin, and Max could feel that her panicked breaths had begun to slow in calming, deep breaths.

"You're safe," he reassured her over and over again until he could feel the tension in her body start to soften. Never in his life had he wanted to kill someone like he had this night, and Heaven help him should he ever see the monster Travertine again.

Pulling one arm from the comforting shield he had formed, he reached for his great coat that had been causally tossed aside earlier. The heavy wool wrapped tight around Bea, helping to build up the needed body heat and chase away the chill that had her shivering in his arms. Soon, they would be seated before a warm fire and he could see to treating her wounds. Bea had her own pride, and the first time she would see herself in a looking glass, Max wanted to be there as support.

Upon account, he could tell that the putrid scum had given her at least one cowardly assault to her face, but there was no telling if he had broken any bones in his attack. Her grip around his back was strong, giving Max the reassurance that her arms and perhaps upper torso were unharmed. He thanked God for arriving when he had and able to stop him from inflicting any other abuse.

Would ever she trust men again?

Would she trust Max?

Her breathing slowed into the smooth, slow rhythm of sleep and Max pushed the questions out of his mind the moment they distracted him, this was not the time to think of his own needs. Max stayed focused on the task at hand. Bea needed him, and he would happily give her whatever the heavens called for to heal his beautiful Bea.

Chapter 4

A Crackling fire and cool compress soothed her burning face, and Bea could feel her sore body being pulled back to the world of the living. Blinking away the darkness of sleep, she welcomed the warm glow of the fireplace and the loving face of her dearest friend looking down on her.

Delicate, shaking fingers reached up to touch Max's face, rough from the nightly growth that she and all other ladies who had managed to avoid his bedchamber had never witnessed. He had always been proud in his need for cleanliness and order, but in this moment, the compulsive thoughts that tended to harm his peaceful nights no longer held importance to him. Bea knew him well and was warmed to know that she held his focus; she was eager to see where this would go.

Smiling up at him, she winced from the pounding pain in her face and shoulders, and was reminding what she must look like to him at this moment. This was not how she would want him to imagine her when they at last took this iconic step. Too important to have this memory tainted, she feared that he would only ever see her now as a victim, and something she most certainly didn't need was a lover who pitied her.

Putting two hands firmly on his chest, she put aside her need for his comfort and chose instead to face this all head on. No man wanted a beaten and battered face to kiss, nor did anyone want a lover who pitied them, Bea saw no hope for them this night and perhaps ever.

Retreating from her without any resistance, he leaned back from her. Pain was creased on his brow, but his eyes glowed in the firelight with understanding. Overwhelmed by his true humanity, Bea wondered how she could have ever mistaken him for a cad. Suddenly, she was taken aback with memories of those same eyes looking at her that first night after she had stormed away from him at the ball and again the day of her wedding. He had always been there, even sitting with her dear Thomas, pouring him brandy while she was behind doors birthing their two children. Max was the second man to hold her babies.

Alone at the gravesite, she would never forget that same look of understanding and comfort as Max offered her his arm for strength. He had always been there, and yet, somehow she had never seen him. How could someone be so significant in her life? She needed to know the truth from Max… but not like this.

Taking a shaky step toward the fire, Bea looked over her shoulder toward where he sat. Overcoat, vest, and neck cloth had been discarded while she slept, and he sat there in his shirtsleeves with an open collar like some rugged hero in one of her mother's gothic novels. Bea had always known Max to be a handsome man, but tonight he was suddenly transformed; he was a protector. Max appeared to be the kind of man strong enough to fight off any aggression toward her, and in her heart, Bea knew that he would.

"So much has happened this night that I don't know what is real anymore," she started, but already Bea could feel her strength start to give out. Her body had been beaten, and she was weaker than she had originally believed. Turning back to the fireplace, she reached out to the mantel for support, but instead was swept up into Max's strong arms.

"I wish I could tell you only the darkest parts were nothing more than a nightmare, but what good is it if we try to hide from all the pain and darkness in our lives?" His dark eyes looked large and vibrant in the firelight. "You were mine to protect and I failed you," his arms tightened around her, and Bea felt safe and at peace, "but never again. I can promise you that."

He carried her through the study doors and made no hesitation to turn toward the staircase. Bea could feel the tension in his body knotted by guilt over what had happened to her that night and she knew there was nothing she could say to ease his mind. Every woman hopes to have a mutual love and respect between herself and her lover, but Bea was practical and knew that between them it would always be out of guilt and obligation to her dead husband. This was not her ideal path to win his heart, but in her beaten and battered state, Bea was desperate for her friend's gentle comfort, and she would happily take whatever he was willing to offer her.

Climbing the stairs with ease, he never once paused or showed himself tiring. Max was a much stronger man than she had ever noticed, and she knew now that with him she was safe, but could she be enough for him?

Stepping from the staircase, Max stopped at the first door on the right. A sliver of warm light broke through the chamber door that stood ajar, inviting Max and Bea into its comforting warmth. Pushing it open with his shoulder, Max carried her into his male sanctuary where she imagined many had passed through before her.

Crossing to the bed, Max carefully laid Bea down over the bedding on the opposite side from where the linen had been turned down already. He remained in his partly undressed state, but made no move to complete the task nor did he show any intention of relieving Bea of her gown. Here she was safe, and he made every intention of helping her to understand that.

Leaving Bea alone on the bed, Max walked over to the fireplace. Facing the fire, Bea observed how the orange glow of the firelight highlighted his broad shoulders and strong legs. He was more than pleasing to look at for Bea, and she figured many women would feel the same.

"I saw you first," his warm voice broke the silence of the room, "He might have been the one to claim you, but I was the one who first saw you."

Bea couldn't figure what he was confessing to her, but her body hurt too much, and she was too distracted by being in Max's chamber and his bed.

"You were the bell of the season," he continued. "Other men might have seen you make your entrance, but I was the one who watched every bounce, step, and nervous flip of your fan. You were a vision, and I wasted no time in obtaining introduction."

"I don't understand?" Trying to sit up, she kept her focus on Max. He turned around and saw her struggle to grab a pillow to keep warm. "Why drag up an unpleasant memory? I knew that night what your first impression was of me from the first time you made a comment regarding my petticoat. I should have thanked you later for that inappropriate comment, for it was Thomas defending my honor that set the path for my future marriage."

"It was all a lie." His words hovered in the room with the escaping smoke from the fire screen.

Twisting and knotting, Bea could feel her stomach turn inside out with fear and apprehension from Max's implied confession. Pulling her legs under, Bea was gaining her strength back at a quicker pace now that they had opened lines of communication.

"When I first danced with you, I was so enchanted by your beauty and your laugh that I needed something… a token to take away with me that night until I could gain something more intimate."

Pulling the cursed handkerchief from his pants pocket, he held it up with one hand, studying it in the fire light. From Bea's view, the orange and yellow fire lit the white handkerchief, capturing all the light, giving it a golden glow in his hand. It looked like he held a ball of golden fire, and Bea wondered how often he had stood at that very fireplace holding her handkerchief.

He sighed softly, holding the linen to his face and sniffing it. "It was my knight's favor from the lady fair, but has long ago lost your sweet scent."

Stunned in silence, she watched as her dearest and truest friend confessed his darkest secrets. That night, she had left the ball fearing that Max would act as a barrier between her and Thomas out of spite, but this revelation was changing history. Bea was afraid to listen to anymore, but couldn't break herself away from this moment.

"It was Thomas," he said turning to her. She couldn't help but notice the bitterness in his voice. "He was the one who asked for my permission to pursue you." Taking slow, calculated steps toward the bed, Bea couldn't make out his facial features, but the firelight highlighted his hair and shoulders.

Distracted from watching his muscular arms move under the fall of his white shirtsleeves and the warm light highlighted his form under the fine linen, Bea's mouth went dry thinking back to the theatre and that storeroom. Was it his intention all along to ask her to be his mistress tonight? Was that the reason for misleading her and setting Lord Travertine aside? She had been beaten this night and hated herself for choosing such a life out of desperation, but a life without Max scared her. She would be willing to be his hidden scandal if it meant he would disrobe and come to bed, never leaving her side again.

"Why bring up all these old memories that will no doubt just open old wounds?" Looking up to what she hoped were the location of his eyes, Bea tried to swallow down her need to hear what was left of his confession to make room for the possibility of their union.

"No this must be said. Far too much time has passed, and I have missed out on a life that I should have had." Taking the remainder steps to her, he kneeled down on the floor beside the bed. "I acted the cad so that Thomas could rescue you. It was all a game, but I willingly partook because I could see the spark of love in his eyes, and I knew that Thomas was the only man I was willing to lose you too." Looking down at the dirty favor, he pinched the most recent bloodstain between his fingers. "Thomas never knew how I felt, he was the better man, and your life was better for it. If only he had lived."

"Those had been my cousin's idea." Bea's smile brightened at the memory, "They were some fantasy idea we had. Something about finding our knights in shining armor and these were our favors that we had made to give to our chosen beau during our first season. When I had tried to retrieve it later that night in order to offer it to Thomas, I figured that it had slipped out earlier that night, I never imagined that you had taken it."

Reaching out, she wrapped her hand around his, encasing the linen between their palms. There was so much more she wanted to tell him, but now seemed too soon and risky. Never had she imagined she could confess such a tale to Max, but after hearing something so heartfelt, and if this had been before Thomas' death, they would have laughed it away, but since she donned the widow's tweed, Max had transformed from Thomas' cad friend to her dearest companion, and now, confidant.

"Before he sailed, Thomas had asked that I watch over you and the boys, and should anything befall him on the voyage, that I take you to wife." Turning his face to meet hers, the light finally caught his face, and she could see the torment in his pinched brow.

Bea's heart dropped, and she felt all the hope and strength leave her body. She was only a widow to be pitied out of devotion to his friend.

"And that is why you..." Swallowing back the pain, she tried to choose her words carefully. "The theatre was only your way of sealing a deal to honor a vow you made to Thomas?" It was all too painful and humiliating to think of, but she couldn't find the will to turn away from him and instead kept looking in to the dead of his eyes.

"No," he rushed to stop her, "That was never part of any bargain or deal. You have been my ideal since that night at the ball, and there is no other I could ever want as I wasn't you." Pulling one hand free from hers, he placed his on top and pulled her hands to his lips. Slowly he placed a kiss on her knuckles and looked deeply into her eyes. "There is no one, but as being Thomas' widow, it pains me to ask this of you..."

"I understand," she rushed; afraid she would lose her nerve if she waited any longer. This was a step down from a ship builder's wife, but she would do whatever she needed to keep Max. "And I accept."

"You do?" His voice brightened, and his eyes sparked to life.

"Of course, but I only ask that we not tell the boys."

"Of course, I would respect your decisions with your children, but I do not understand how that would be possible? How can you keep such a thing a secret when we are all living under the same roof?"

Pulling her hands away, she folded them in her lap, trying to gain her composure.

"The same roof?" she repeated. "But that is not customary, as I have been led to believe."

"Customary?" Tilting his head to the side, he looked perplexed. "I know it will be hard for you to move on after losing Thomas, and I will strive to be understanding at all turns in the road, but I must insist that my wife and godsons reside in the same home as I do."

"Your wife?" she stuttered.

"Yes, my wife." Shaking his head trying to understand where this conversation had gone, "What do you think you just agreed to?"

"To be your mistress," she confessed with shame.

Dropping his head, Bea could see the first roll of laughter in his shoulders before any chuckle escaped his mouth. Embarrassed and ashamed for thinking that he had no honor in his proposal, Bea sat in silence and hoped that he would forgive her.

"You thought I wanted you as my mistress?" Looking back up at her, his laughter died away, and despite the smile that stretched across his face, she could see the pain in his eyes. Reaching up, he let loose of the handkerchief and gently held her face in his hands. "Why would I want to cheapen what we could have and why would I want to cheat myself from the joy of growing old with you? Don't ever doubt my feelings for you. You are the only woman I have ever loved, and I never want to feel shame for my heart's desire again."

Pulling her to him, he kissed her long and hard. Bea melted in his arms and felt the room start to spin around her. His kisses chased away what doubts she had and filled her with the warmth of his tenderness.

Laying her back onto the pillows, Bea could feel the shifting in the mattress when he kneeled onto the side of the bed. There were no thoughts of Thomas, and though she knew the guilt might follow in the morning, there was none felt now. Instead, Bea felt free to enjoy his masculine scent and strong arms around her.

Lifting his head, he looked down into her eyes with tenderness that almost brought Bea to tears. He was so gentle, yet so powerful. She didn't know for sure what to think at this moment, other than how desperately she needed him. His eyes shifted to her cheek and the bite marks on her lip. He was looking at her battered face and not at the lips he longed to kiss. Shrugging away, Bea wanted to hide and pray he would forget how she looked that night. In time, all her bruises would fade and her lip would heal, but until then, she thought that this night might have to wait.

Rolling in his arms onto her side, Bea faced the center of the bed and cupped her hands over her face. She did not want to distort his image of her, hoped he would understand, and simply drift off to sleep. Bea never held such luck.

"Why do you turn from me?" He sat up on his knees and gently held her by the shoulders, turning Bea to face him. Her hand did not move from their shielded position until he unwrapped her face -one hand at a time- holding them on either side of her face. "You have no reason to hide from me." His protests suddenly ceased to make way for a couple curses under his breath, "You fear me don't you?"

"Fear you?" Such an idea was absurd.

"Because of my behavior at the theatre, you fear me for how I treated you in tying you to that chair..."

"I swear that fear is the last thing I feel when I think of that," she blurted out before she realized the words were out. Despite the dramas of this night, he was still her friend; there was a part of her that still felt at ease with him. "Thomas was not much of an adventurer in those matters, but he did at times speak of his youthful days with you, and I have to say, I was always curious." She paused to remind herself where she was after speaking to Max with open ease, as though this were just another night in her library. "No, you have nothing to apologize for. In fact, perhaps the subject might be revisited in the future?"

Tension fell away from Max in one deep breath.

"But then why do you hide from me?" he asked softly.

"How can you make love to a beaten woman?" she asked, fighting away the tears that had now begun to fall down her cheeks.

Leaning down, Max kissed her right tear soaked cheek and then her eye. His kisses were feather light, drawing Bea up to him, making her want to open up to him completely, but she was still afraid.

"You have tried to hide your face from me ever since I lifted you into my carriage, and it is futile and pointless." Leaning down, he kissed her left cheek followed by her matching eye. His warm lips soothed her and Bea desperately wanted him to keep going, but she couldn't let go of her pride. "Do you not see that none of this matters to me? Your bruises are only temporary, and in time, looks do fade; twenty years from now, when I am potbellied and bald, I might shrug away from you, and when I do I hope that you will say the same thing I tell you now. 'I love the person you are underneath; everything else is just a bonus dressing.'" He was a wise man, and he loved her.

He loved her!

Bea was stunned that she hadn't processed this yet. In one night, she had gone from having nothing to having everything, and it was all thanks to one man declaring his love for her.

"Will you help me undress?" she asked him

Perhaps it was a bit bold, but if she didn't make the leap over that first step, she feared that the courage to move forward would never come.

Lying on her stomach, Bea melted when he unbuttoned the four cloth covered buttons and kissed her gently between her shoulders. Warm breath and strong lips burned an imprint on her skin. Next, came the line of hooks so he could spread open the back of her ball gown. Slowly, he spread the gown apart, revealing to him the bowed ties that cinched her in. Pulling the cords out of the tie, Bea let go of a deeply held breath that she did not know she had been holding. The corset ties proved to be another obstacle that Max enjoyed.

Warm strong hands worked their way between Bea and her gown, reaching down until they rested flat on her stomach. Bea's heart was beating madly, and her skin was flushed. Heated and wet, her sex was throbbing, weeping at his touch, but he did nothing for a moment other than hold his hands in place. He leaned forward and pulled her back into his chest. Warm and inviting, she felt confident in this and all fears and reservations washed away.

Biting the bottom of her ear lobe, he said not a word, but grunted and groaned, sounds that hummed through her tingling body.

"Max," the words escaped her lips on a breath.

"Shh," he instructed as he began to unhook the front of her corset, starting with the top and working his way down.

Large, strong hands reached under the top of Bea's corset to pull her breasts free of the loosened restraint. Kneading and massaging the tender orbs, Bea was short of breath for wanting. He was the second man to have ever touched her in such a way, and though she had loved her husband dearly and treasured every erotic memory of them together, there was something different, something forbidden and yet irresistible about Max. Rolling her head back on his shoulder, she followed his guide as he pulled her up onto her knees, letting her gown and corset fall from her body, exposing her to the warm room. His hands left her for only a moment to pull his linen shirt off over his head. The sizzling feeling of his naked front connecting to her bare back ran through her blood, awakening every nerve to the sensation.

"My dearest Bea," his breath was coming out in short pants, and his voice was deep with lust, "I have waited so long for this moment, you are all my dreams come true."

Spinning Bea around, he laid her back down on the pillows, and standing up to pull her dress from her legs, he walking over to toss it into the fire. Gasping out of horror, she watched her dress ignite in a quick blast before it turned in on itself- shriveling into a black mess of ash. It had been a shameful piece of muslin, and after tonight, it was perhaps torn and stained beyond repair, but this left her with nothing to wear home in the morning. What would her boy nurse think when she does not return due to lack of clothing?

"You are too beautiful to wear such black memories." Walking back to her, he released the top button of his trousers with this right hand and stopped there, hooking his thumb in the loosened waistline. Taking one more step and stopping when his knees touched the mattress, he looked down at her and smiled. "I look forward to creating new memoirs for us to share for many years to come."

Lying before him naked, she felt beautiful. His eyes ran along her body, up and down, and sparkling with a satisfaction for the gift before him. She was starting to grow impatient and wanted to move this night along. Her body had been burning for his for far too long, and he simply did not move fast enough for her tastes. Sitting up on her heels, she reached out with both hands to release the remaining buttons, pulling the front open to allow his erection to spring forward. Running her hands under the backside of his trousers, she pushed them down, over his round posterior, and held him firmly in her soft lady hands.

The only benefit in being a widow was her lack of fear this time around. This time she knew what to expect, and she knew what she liked. If only she could get the images from the opera house out of her mind and concentrate on the here and now.

"Tell me if this is still too soon?" Holding her face in his hands, he did not move to remove her hand from him, and his words were honest and sincere. "I can wait for when you are ready, but I will not stand as substitute for my friend."

Gripping his backside firmly, she pulled him closer to her, crushing her breasts against his chest. His tall frame separated them, and she straightened up, trying to meet him face to face, but still, she had to look up at him. His face looked confidant and handsome, as it always did, but his eyes betrayed him and showed his pain and fear.

"I love you Sir Edmond Maximums Dubershire the Third, and there is no other man I want to be with." She spoke from the heart and felt a great weight being lifted. "You have become my dearest friend and confidant, and I beg you now to make me yours." Running one hand up his back, she let the other venture around his waist to over his strong abdomen. Rippled with muscles, her fingers follow a trail down over his flat belly where his throbbing erection stood proud. He was long, thick, and felt good in her hand. Max hissed out a breath, which made Bea smile for the power she had over him at this moment. Gripping her hand tightly around his base, she slid her fingers up toward the tip and back down. "Be my lover and my husband."

Crushing his lips to hers, Max kissed her with a fierce passion that she quickly met. Arms wrapped around each other, his trousers fell quickly to the ground, freeing him of any other restraint and opening the doors to new passions, new pleasures, and a new life.

Biography
Eryn Black

A California girl to her core Eryn was born in East L.A. and raised by her inspirational and talented mother in Sierra Madre, California (hidden above the rosy city of Pasadena). There she indulged herself in reading Anne of Green Gables, The Scarlet Pimpernel and Ivanhoe under the California sun, but she never had any interest in the romance genera beyond the classics. Then one long lonely night a few years ago she came across a friends discarded paperback romance and she has been hooked ever since. A lover of reading and a lover of… well… just a lover Eryn has taken on this new adventure in her life putting pen to paper and digging deep to reveal all of the delightful and erotic stories that have tormented her dreams. Eryn hopes that you will enjoy reading her adventures as much as she has enjoyed writing them.

Check out Eryn's website for any future releases
www.erynblack.com

Enjoy this preview of

With This Ring

Present Day San Francisco

Fog rolled into the bay early that day, sealing the city in a thick layer of damp cold. All along Fisherman's Wharf, couples held each other close, exchanging body heat in the form of hands, arms and lips. After a record breaking cold winter, Sasha was enjoying the opportunity to wear a lightweight leather jacket instead of her less than flattering parka. A half empty bottle of penicillin rattled in her pocket as a reminder of the cold she had had last year when he refused to call in sick to work and take care of her. He never took care of her when she was sick or in need of comfort, but that particular time should have been foretelling to her of what was to come. Nursing a broken heart in one of the most romantic cities in the world was like a doctor using a fishing hook to sew up a patient after surgery. There was little hope for Sasha that night to find peace, and alone she settled on buying herself an Irish coffee at her favorite bar.

Over her shoulder, Sasha took in the dramatic view once more. Seagulls flew through the thick fog and the masts of the tall ships docked at the tourist site disappeared into the grey atmosphere. The iconic Golden Gate Bridge was a phantom shadow in the distance where only the headlights of cars crossing over could be seen. Lost in the signature fog, San Francisco was indeed a city for lovers, and here Sasha walked alone on her birthday while her ex-fiancé was finding solace in the arms of Jessica- an intern he had been screwing behind her back for the last four months.

A flash of heat hit her face when Sasha opened the glass door. Warm and filled with jovial bodies enjoying their drinks and clam chowder after a long day of work or sightseeing. Built in the 1890's, The Buena Vista was one of the oldest bars in the city and breathed nostalgia from the worn floorboards to the wood carved bar. Tourists sat on barstools watching the bartender line up 6 of their signature glasses in a row, dropping a cube of sugar in each he then poured in the steaming hot coffee, cream, and their own personal whiskey. Rising to the top, the cream created a frothy head while the steam from the coffee escaped, patrons applauded his skill at the famous pour and eagerly received their Irish coffee's.

"Sasha!" over the cheers and laughter she heard a familiar voice call out to her. "Over here! Sasha!" Again he called out.

With a tilt of her head to the right and then the left, Patrick's nut brown curls finally came into view. Two hands reached up over people's heads each holding a hot steaming glass of whiskey filled coffee, cream sloshed around the rim of one when he waved his hand in her direction, bidding Sasha to join him.

A defeated sigh was her answer to finally accepting his invitation for an after work drink. In the one month he had worked at her office, Patrick had invited Sasha out for drinks nearly every day. For the last week he had joined her for salads and sandwiches during their lunch break and she had been surprised at how natural their first conversation had flowed, but Sasha was nursing a broken heart on her birthday and didn't feel up to entertaining anyone that night.

Ten slow steps of pushing and squeezing past the flux of people felt more like a wrestling match, but Sasha made it across the bar to Patrick where he had one empty bar stool available next to him. A coveted seat, Sasha watched him set down the drinks to shoo away a couple of people holding the seat for her. She left her jacket on, but standing up, he insisted on taking her coat for her. Black leather was a fashion statement she should have left in the 90's, but she liked the look of her black slacks, red sweater and black high heels. It was a powerful look with a bit of dominance to it and she blended in well with the rest of the 9-5 work crowd in there.

"What are you doing here?" Sasha asked, trying to focus the direction of her voice toward him, fighting against the constant rumble of conversations.

"Ever'one should enjoy a good drink at the end of a long week." His Irish accent added a charming endearment to him. If Vince hadn't severed her trust in men, Sasha could see how she would find Patrick attractive.

Standing at 6'2" with wide shoulders over a narrow body, he looked like a man who lived a fit life. Dressed down a bit for the office, he tended to wear more jeans, than slacks with his dress shirts, but as a transfer from overseas, there was a lot of leeway given to him for being from out of the country. Coming to them with little to no computer skills the rumors were that he was the nephew to the CEO, but despite his lack of ability his charm and friendliness did bring a moral boost to her department.

"I thought your people drank beer?" She joked with him.

"If thar' were true this here," he gestured to his glass, "Would be called a San Francisco coffee," he remarked, "but ye make a good point, I do love a good dark pint." His eyes lit up when he smiled and for the first time that day, Sasha felt some of the weight fall off her shoulders and she was relaxing.

"Please join me." he invited her. Smooth, clean-shaven cheeks pressed up in his face, pulling the corners of his mouth and narrowing his eyes into a warm smile. The moment Sasha slid onto the barstool, she knew that she had succeeded in making a number of women in the bar jealous.

They held their glasses up and she let the warmth of the hot coffee seep into her hands. A ring from the lip of his glass clinking against hers surprised Sasha and she turned her head to see a pair of sincere steel blue eyes looking into hers. Sasha nervously swallowed and tried to will her hand to move, but she was frozen in the spot, locked in the spell of his eyes.

"Blessings on yer' birthday." His melodic accent massaged her lonely soul, but the toast drew her back to the present, breaking the spell.

Sasha felt the heat of blood rushing to her cheeks and looked down at the glossy, polished wood bar, awkwardly avoiding him as best she could. Happy birthday's had always embarrassed her, but today they only made her want to run to the restroom and cry in private. For the first time that day she'd heard someone give her the wish as a friendly gesture that was not laced with the pity and empathy knowing she would be spending this birthday single and alone.

"Thank you," She said feeling her face form into the first true and honest smile she had felt in days.

He was the first to move the glass to his lips, but he held it there waiting for her to follow suit. The cool glass pressed against her lips, followed quickly by the hot steam of the drink swirling up and tickling her nose. The thick smell of whiskey wafted to her head and Sasha parted her lips, inviting the first taste. Thick cream first filled her mouth followed by the hot sweet coffee, it was a smooth sensation that relaxed Sasha in her seat. Closing her lips over the rim of the glass, she swiped her tongue over the beveled edge of the glass enjoying the contrast of hot and cold, then the taste of warm, strong whiskey dominated her senses and soothed her chest with a deep burn.

"Hmm," she sighed, setting her glass down, keeping her fingers protectively linked around the stem of the glass with her wrists resting comfortably on the bar. The whiskey worked its magic and soon the loud chatter and laughter of twenty or more conversations lulled into a melodic mumble, it was still difficult to hear Patrick's voice, but the frustration had slipped by.

"Yer nut much o'a drinker are ye?" his accent

was charming and for the first time he was no longer that cheerful puppy who followed her around the office. In the change from fluorescent office lights to the warmer glow of the bar lanterns and chandelier she felt softer and more feminine. Cut with a casual length, his hair curled at the top nearly an inch too long for the typical conservative men she passed by in her daily life, but the sides were clean and sculpted around his face in a relaxed, but clearly expensive cut.

"I skipped lunch and this tastes," looking down at her empty glass, Sasha was amazed to see that she had already finished her drink, "or tasted, so good."

She sighed again when she licked the sweet cream from her tingling lips and took no notice of Patrick signaling the bartender for another round. The older gentleman smiled when he replaced the two empty glasses in front of them and began to perform his signature pour for them. His gray hair was cut short and he wore a long sleeve button-down shirt, a white apron – that despite all the coffee served were both pristine white- and a black bow tie, dressed from another time he said very little, but sounded almost Bostonian; Sasha wondered if the charming accent of the bartender was all part of the show.

"What shall we drink this one to?" she asked when the bartender smiled and left them alone with their drinks.

"To new adventures." They toasted their glasses together again and Sasha was amazed at how relaxed she felt.

All the pain and sorrow from the past month had fallen away. Never one to drink too much, she was discovering the draw people have to medicate a broken heart with hard alcohol.

"So, Patrick," she popped and licked her lips, enjoying the tingling sensation, "what is your last name?"

"Patrick Gallagher be the name on me name plate at work."

"Gallagher?" Wiping the rim of her glass with her finger, Sasha licked the foam from it, "Any relation to Liam Gallagher the owner of Random Hearts?" She was getting bold in her questions, but she didn't care.

"We are related in a way." He was not willing to say anymore, "But I would appreciate it if you didn't tell anyone."

Sasha, hemmed and hawed at his answer trying to not be so obvious in her realization that he had been employed through nepotism. Handsome and new, he was an easy target for gossip and she hoped that she would be able to keep this little tidbit to herself come Monday morning.

The time passed by quickly for Sasha, sitting at the bar enjoying another two rounds of Irish coffee's and a bowl of clam chowder. They laughed and talked about the city and local sports. He was pleased when she explained the rules behind American football and was pleased when she expressed her dislike for the sport as he shared her opinion. Before long Vince was out of her thoughts completely and when it came time to pay the bill he offered her his arm to lean on.

Cautiously walking out of the bar, Sasha leaned her head on Patrick's shoulder and thought how comfortable and safe she felt with him. Sasha knew she was lucky in finding a new friend at such a dark time in her life. They'd only walked a few steps when he stopped and turned her to a shop window.

"What is it?" She asked lifting her head from his shoulder and looking up at a shop window. Dressed with knick-knacks, porcelain statues and a majestic grandfather clock with a sweet rag doll sitting on the top looking down at her with black button eyes. "It's amazing the turnover with shops around here. It's really sad when you think about it, it was only a couple weeks ago this was a tourist camera shop."

"Like that one," Patrick gestured to the shop next door.

"Yes, wait," squinting her eyes she tried to focus, "That is the shop, but I don't understand?"

looking back and forth from the bar to the camera shop and then the antique shop in between. "I could have sworn that that camera shop was right here," but the truth was standing right in front of her.

"Ye really canna' drink can ye?" The warm drawl of his voice tickled her. He was friendly and sweet.

"I guess not," A giggle rumbled in her, Sasha bit her lips closed to contain it.

'Boy, I have had too much to drink.' Her inner voice critiqued.

Somewhere In Time, the gold lettering read on the window. Scrolled in an elegant calligraphy, the letters were highlighted with bronze and then black on the outside. There was something haunting in the name and old world to the look of the signage. Painted at the foot of the last letter was an open pocket watch with a chain that curled under the shop's name adding a whimsical elegance. Sasha was entranced by the shop and felt herself being pulled toward it.

"Poppin' fer a gander?" Patrick had begun to linger in the background, blending in with passersby and taxies.

Across the street a trolley clanged, coming into the station, but Sasha never took any notice of it, nor did she realize that Patrick had held the door open for her until they were standing in the center of the shop. A low hum, reverberated from her chest, pulling her like a fish on a hook, she didn't know what she was looking for or wanted, but she walked as if her legs were no longer her own.

"It's a quaint shop." he complimented.

"Yes, "Looking around at the wall of cuckoo clocks that all ticked and tocked in a chorus, but none of them pointed at the same time, "But kind of old fashioned. I mean this is tourist central. What is an antique shop doing here?"

Despite her protest in the poor choice of business location, she continued to walk deeper into the shop. Located in the back was a glass counter with a gold plated shell sitting on top, holding a delicate miniature china doll with golden yellow curls, pantaloons, painted black shoes and a blue gingham dress. Sasha reached out to pick the doll up, but was stopped with an invading voice.

"Little Goldie is a charming thing." Crisp and proper, a gentleman's voice came from behind a tall urn standing beside a column. Clean and conservative, he emitted a formal stature, from his properly clipped grey hair, manicured beard that was trimmed close to his face, his three-piece grey pinstriped suit, and gold watch fob that hung across his waistcoat. He held a plaid tartan in one hand, which he carefully draped over the back of a chair for display before he approached them. Slightly wrinkled, his hand reached out to protectively retrieve the doll. Cradled in his hands, her ringlets fell over the back of his hand and he brushed her painted rosy cheeks with the pad of his thumb.

"She's beautiful." Sasha leaned over to get a closer look. "I had one like her when I was a girl."

"Possibly, but this one is very unique. " The man walked around, behind the counter and rejoined them with the glass display case between them. Setting the doll on a mahogany shelf behind him he turned back to Sasha and Patrick with his arms spread out in a friendly greeting. "Allow me to introduce myself, Herbert Well's at your service and welcome to my shop." Reaching into his waistcoat pocket that held the open end of his watch fob Herbert pulled out a white business card. "Is there anything you are interested in seeing?"

Sasha held the card in one hand, it read:

Somewhere In Time

Herbert G. Wells

Antiquities and Fantasies

She was perplexed to see no phone number or address and turned the card over a couple of times to look. Thanking him for the card she slipped it into her pants pocket and realized she had not answered his question.

"I'm not really sure…" Sasha backed away from the counter feeling foolish for walking into a shop with no intent other than to look around.

"Come on *cailin beag*," Patrick encouraged her with a friendly pat to her back, "Everyone should have a birthday present."

Sasha looked from the older gentleman to Patrick and up at the pretty doll.

"Your friend is right," Mr. Wells wiggled his nose and the bristles rustled around his mouth.

Despite his prim and proper appearance and his ramrod stick posture, he was clearly a friendly and approachable man. Sasha felt at ease in his shop and to her surprise wanted to buy herself a birthday present… more than wanted; she needed to buy a present. Looking down into the glass display case that stood as a barrier between her and Mr. Wells Sasha looked at the selection.

"That's lovely," she complimented pointing at a butterfly broach resting on a black velvet cushion, pretty and elegant she could imagine it displayed in her practically empty jewelry box at home, but something didn't seem right in the fit.

"No," she changed her mind shaking her head.

"That's just as well, this item is already spoken for," he said moving the broach from the display case and setting it beside the doll.

Sasha's eyes kept returning to the doll on the shelf, telling herself that she would look perfect on her vanity at home, but despite her interest there was a nagging feeling in her gut telling her to keep looking. Playing a game of Hot and Cold with her senses, she surveyed the display case while a voice in the back of her head told Sasha that she would know what it was when she saw it. Hatpins, earrings, bracelets and cigarette cases flashed by her, but nothing seemed to jump out and say, "Buy me".

"May I suggest a nice necklace?" Mr. Wells offered, but Sasha didn't hear him and kept looking. The rumble of voices told her that he and Patrick were exchanging words in a quiet conversation, but she couldn't make out any of it. Soon the nagging feeling turned to an echoing hum, like a metal detector, encouraging her to move along in her search.

"What about that?" She pointed at a ring sitting on a bed of dried heather.

"The heather suits you, it matches the lavender

in your eyes," Patrick complimented and surprised Sasha in being the first moment he had made such a familiar and intimate observation.

"Not the dried flower," she pointed again, tapping her finger on the glass top, "The ring."

"The Claddagh," the shopkeeper answered, "A fine choice, is this to be an engagement ring?" He looked between the two of them and Sasha felt a flood of emotions with the mistaken standing of her relationship status.

"No," Patrick answered and looked at Sasha's downturned head and smiled, "Not yet," he joked, wrapping his arm around her shoulder and gently shaking her side to side, relaxing Sasha and making light of her recent tragic love life.

"Well then," the shopkeeper started retrieving the ring from inside the display case and setting it in the same gold plated shell that Goldie had been sitting in, "This is a very special ring."

"How so?" Sasha asked, feeling her anxiety begin to ease.

"The Claddagh is also known as the wedding band." His finger traced the front where two hands reached from right and left where they held a heart topped off with a crown. It looked almost regal to Sasha.

"This ring is a simple way to let the lad's know if you are available or if you have been courted by a young lad."

"A relationship status ring?" she laughed.

"In a way," he nodded and picked the ring up to present it to her on his open palm.

Eagerly, Sasha plucked the ring from his hand and started to put it on, but Patrick stopped her with his hand over hers, shielding her hand from the ring.

"This is not just a ring ye can pu' on." He warned her.

"How would you know?" She asked pulling her hand out of his reach.

"It's an Irish ring and has an ancient tradition." He warned her. "Mr. Wells, perhaps ye can explain' to the *Cailin*."

"Yes, well," he cleared his throat and combed his fingers through the short hairs on his beard, "It is in the heart, when the heart is pointed toward you, you have been claimed by your love, but when it is turned away from you, you're still free to be courted."

Sasha thought for a moment how easy it would be to wear this ring and tell her family that she was taken without producing a man. She didn't know when or if she would be able to trust her heart again to someone, but this could give her some peace and quiet for a while. Turning the ring around she started to slide it on, but this time it was Mr. Wells who stopped her.

"It is important that you hold true to the ring, it is one thing to lie to those around you, but you tempt fate when you lie to your own heart."

His warning was a challenge for her. Inserting her finger into the center of the brass ring she felt a shock spark hit the tip of her finger and retreated her hand from the ring for a moment, looking up into Patrick's concerned eyes. Perhaps it was his Irish upbringing that made him so superstitious, but she wasn't about to let a ring intimidate her. Stubborn and determined she tried again, stabbing her finger through the ring and ignoring the sharp pain of static electricity that sealed the band at the base of her finger.

Violent stinging sparks burst from the ring, shocking Sasha who backed away from the counter and reached to pull the ring from her finger. Ribbons of electric light sprung from the ring like a violent man eating plant, whipping around and latching to her fingers, hand and arm. She pulled at the ring with all her might, but it held tight and soon the sparks began to merge and encase her hands in light.

Desperate in her panic, Sasha looked up to Patrick and Mr. Wells for help, but they were in conversation and oblivious to her plight. She screamed out for them her voice ricocheted around the growing cage of sparks that was now consuming her, entrapping her voice. Quickly, the light of the shop fell away into darkness and she felt herself pulled from the two men at the counter, propelled down a long corridor of blackness in the electrified cocoon until they were nothing more than a small dot of light that vanished among thousands of stars above her.

Burning into her finger, the ring grafted itself to the skin. Both her hands were locked together, secured by the restraints of the incandescent blue sparks. Her screams were absorbed into the cage and she felt a melodic ringing that canceled out any noise from the outside. Space flashed by her and soon she no longer felt as if she were being pulled, but rather falling. Feet first, she spun around like a top, building up momentum. Looking down, the earth grew at her feet while it spun around like a cyclone and she sensed her impending doom.

Just as quickly as the terror captured her, Sasha fell free from her cocoon safely on a thick bed of barley, clover, and cornflowers. The bright light of her cocoon fell away and Sasha was left in the black of night with millions of stars above her and the largest full moon she had ever seen lighting the landscape in silver light.

York March 1853

Rain flooded the countryside, threatening to suffer the roads and farms that the county had not known in a generation, and all of this on Beth's Wedding day. To prevent being muddied and sullen, she had been forced to step from the carriage onto planks of wood that floated over the mud and rain runoff. Even with the assistance of her poorly laden bridge, Beth still managed to lose one shoe in the mud when her footing slipped. She was cold, wet, filthy, and about to face a man she had danced with only once: a man who in a short time would be her husband.

This day it was not just the rain that dripped from her cheeks, but tears. Empty seats greeted Beth when she walked through the double doors. The only person in attendance was her mother, seated in the front pew, ready for her daughter to make her long awaited marriage. The emptiness was just a reminder of the man she was to wed, making her feel like a dirty secret being past off to the quickest bidder while no one was watching.

This was not the fairytale marriage she had dreamed about, but instead her day had turned to a nightmarish scene from one Beth's gothic novels that she kept tucked under her pillow. Only this time the handsome hero would not come riding up to rescue her at the last moment... There was no hero in her future.

Dark hair and darker eyes, Beth was more frightened by her husband to be than she had been at their first introduction. He was a head taller than her, and his eyes were shadowed by his prominent brow, giving him a permanent expression of disdain. His jaw was square and much like a marble statue-cold and perfect. Any woman would say, without a doubt, that Charles Constantine Fairchild, the Fifth Earl of Blythe, or Connie to his friends, was a handsome man, but what could she say for the man beneath the facade? Keeping her eyes focused on the diamond stickpin that was tucked in the pillowy, white fluff of his dry and elegant cravat. She had given it to him the night their engagement had been announced, but his thank you had been lost in his quick request for her father's forgiveness in not being prepared with any token to present in exchange. Standing now with her naked finger, Beth could feel a straining grip around her heart that she couldn't seem to escape from.

"You may kiss the bride." The pastor made the dreaded announcement and that was the moment when Beth noticed that she had been wool gathering. Blushing to a quirked grin the pastor gave her, Beth turned to her now husband only to stutter at the hardened expression he branded her with.

"Excuse me." Biting her bottom lip she closed her eyes and imagined herself standing before an execution squad.

"No need," he whispered. His deep voice ran down her spine and left her legs trembling. The smell of brandy stung her senses and slapped away what hope she had been reaching for. He had met her at the altar pickled, numbing himself from whatever he had been suppressing since the night of their first and only waltz.

Gripping the hairs at the back of her neck, her new husband, lord and master pulled her to him and into a scandalous kiss that dominated her lips. Sucking her lower lip free of her teeth, he pulled her in, and for what felt like an eternity, he scandalously devoured her before her parents and the local pastor who had baptized her as a babe.

Then it was over.

Releasing her from the kiss, the Earl of Blythe turned to his new father in-law and shook his hand. He then thanked the pastor for the service before slipping a few extra coins in the offertory box.

"We would be honored if you will join us back at our home where we have prepared a wedding breakfast. There you will be able to meet Beth's other sisters..." but Beth's father was cut off by her husband's stern look, and staggering he reached out to steady himself on the back of a nearby pew.

"I fear that there is no time. I am expected in London by tonight and I cannot be delayed much longer." His refusal was a sharp strike to the gentleman's pride.

Pulled away from her father's reply, Beth was dragged away from the parents she loved, through the doors of the church, and out into the rain. Connie was crowned with a tall hat that helped protect him from the rainfall, but she was left exposed as he rushed her down the steps and into the waiting carriage.

With her hair falling limp from the weight of the rain- that now dripped from her head to toe- Beth tried to fight off the urge to burst into tears. She was devastated that she had just been rushed through the most important ceremony of her young life and could not recall a moment of it, being lost in her daydreams and dread.

"Damn!" His booming voice awoke her from her wallowing. Pealing his wet coat off, he tried to wipe the beading drops of rain off the black wool. Beth looked on in shock, shivering in her wet and cold condition.

"Lean forward," he demanded. Not waiting for her to act, he guided her shoulders forward and draped the coat over her.

Warmed by his body heat that still filed the lining, Beth felt that she should be grateful, but could not find the polite words, seeing how she was still stunned at his treatment toward her on their wedding day. If not for the overwhelming amount of shock, perhaps the carriage ride would have been different. She couldn't find the voice to fight back at his actions and demand what she knew full well she deserved on this day.

"Thank you." Hating the week quiver in her voice, Beth bit her bottom lip for fear of embarrassing herself with more crying. She had shed enough tears this day.

"At least the bricks have been warmed." Stretching his legs out before him he tried to get comfortable, but his tall build could not unfold completely. "That will make our journey a bit more livable." Tipping his hat over his eyes, shielding himself from her glaring eyes, he folded his arms over his chest and nestled into the back of the seat. "You had best try and get some rest. We have a significant amount of road to cover before we can take the time to make our first stop."

Perhaps his words would have been more clearer if not for his voice being drowned out by the very un-lady like rumble of her empty stomach.

"When do you think we will stop to break our fast?" Cursing the well trained politeness in her when he deserved no such thing, Beth folded her hands in front of her rumbling tummy, hoping to drown out the humiliating sound.

"I fear there is no time for us to stop until we take a late lunch. I had assumed that your maid had properly served you something this morning?"

"I was too nervous to eat, and knowing that the wedding breakfast was to follow, I did not worry about my morning tray."

"Will I hear nothing else this day beyond that cursed farce of a breakfast?" he snapped. "This is not a celebration princess..." Reaching into his inside breast pocket he pulled out a silver flask, etched with a clover circled by filigree, he drained what little was left. Wiping his mouth dry, he pocketed the empty flask and gestured to the rain covered glass of the carriage window. "There are heated bricks in the floor for your comfort, we have no time to dally on the road or else there will be no hope of us making it home in time."

Home? It sounded foreign coming from him. Still in shock from the saddest wedding Beth had ever attended, she was at a loss to comprehend the idea that she was now bound to this man, body and -heaven forbid- soul. They were strangers that had been victims to a marriage contract that their grandfathers had shaken hands on over a card game when she was only a month old. Desperate to save their daughter from the old man's willingness to play with other people's lives, her parents had done whatever was humanly possible to fight this contract, but in the end, the old man won. Adding a stipulation to his will, her grandfather managed to deny her a proper dowry that would be financed through the estate. She had been humbled before her family and left to the will of a man who was now buried six feet under.

Sitting as the sacrificial lamb being taken away to the altar with an empty belly, Beth's mind kept wandering back to the first time she had seen her now husband. He presenting himself formally at the last ball of the season, requesting her hand in a waltz. He had been a dream, charming and debonair, able to sweep her off her feet in a single dance. She had laughed at his witty conversation. He had made her feel not only intelligent, but desirable- something that she had never felt in a man's company before. Caught up in all the romance of the night, she had fallen fast and hard when her mother told her of her family's betrayal.

Pulling the lapel of his overcoat around her neck she tried to shield herself from the cold of her marriage and her now snoring travel companion; his arms folded across his chest and his ankles crossed on the seat across them. There was more room in her husband's carriage then she had previously assumed and that if there had been a basket to settle her growling stomach, then perhaps she could have found peace on their journey. Leaning her head back against the seat she closed her eyes, yielded to the roll of the carriage and the warmth of the leftover body heat that wrapped around her in his coat-laced with a combined scent of sandalwood and something else, something intoxicating that she took in over and over again until at last she drifted off to sleep.

The rain had not lightened up when Beth opened her eyes. Limbs still and her neck aching, she tried to roll her arms and head to stretch out the snap and pop left from her nap. Looking to her right, she saw her husband was taking advantage of the time to sleep off whatever had left him in such a foul mood that morning. Gray skies overhead kept her from knowing how long she had slept, but by going from the stiff, binding pain of her shoulders, she hoped that they would be arriving in London soon, but that was unlikely.

Stretching her legs in front of her with a groan, she kicked an obstruction on the floor. Looking down, Beth found her feet had collided into a small basket. Beth could not ignore the smells that were escaping between he wicker weave and reached down to lift the lid. Growls escaped her very empty stomach when she saw the paper wrapped items that smelled like fresh meat pies. She knew that he must have made an unscheduled stop while she slept to get her something to eat.

Dropping the lid, she turned to her new husband in a rush of graduated, but the rush was quickly gone when she saw the half empty bottle of brandy that hung loosely in his fingers. He had taken the only escape he could find from the awkward carriage ride, and his lustful sandalwood scent was washed out by the stinging stench of alcohol. Giving the basket a good kick, she threw herself into her corner of the carriage and folded her arms in a huff; her dreams of a love match had already been ripped away by this sham of a wedding, now only to be capped off with a husband unable to sustain a carriage ride with her sober.

Anger did not chase away the hunger pains, and when she noticed that, no matter the bumps in the road, Beth surrendered to her needs and bit into the flaky crust of the meat pie. Licking the dripping gravy from her lower lip and chin, she melted into the filling taste. At last there was something to her liking this day. It was not the wedding breakfast that she had been expecting, with course after course of her father's elegant menu and was something she had looked forward to sharing with the company of her two dearest friends and sisters. Not allowed to attend the wedding out of the demands of her new husband, she desperately missed their companionship this day.

"A small wedding is what I must insist on," he told her father a week ago, "Something that will not attract too much attention. The sooner this whole thing is done with the better."

Beyond that one dance, he had not paid her a moment's notice until that heated kiss at the altar. The hairs at the base of her neck still stung from the way he had gripped her, and every time she remembered the thrill of the dominate kiss, goose flesh rose on her arms and her corset tightened around her breasts. There was so much about her new husband that infuriated her and frightened her, but it was her body that had truly betrayed her.

Brushing the crumbs from her, she risked one more glance at her husband. He remained undisturbed in his drunken sleep, so she continued to enjoy her very late meal and lifted another meat pie from the basket. The second was better than the first and she thanked Heaven he was not awake to witness her gluttony.

A dead man couldn't sleep after seeing his wife lick droplets of gravy from her lips and fingers. She had a mouth that could tempt a monk. Connie had been hoping that his cramped pose would conceal the raging erection that had been tormenting him since that blasted kiss. She had been so pliable in his arms, melting to his touch, and surrendering to his lips. This was not how it was supposed to be! A wife is for breeding and nothing more, and any man who believes otherwise was a fool.

Trying, to hold tight to he bottleneck for fear of dropping it and admitting to his bride that he was awake and be forced to face her in a conversation. Born from his own actions, he did not deny his cowards state and continued to snore in his own drunken shame. Intending for the basket to be a peace offering, he had instructed his man to stop at the first inn they passed to find his bride some sustenance, but now her delights in the tavern food was becoming his agony. Need and lust were growing, and his restraint was nearly boiling over. She popped the last bite into her mouth and returned to the sinful licking her fingers. No man fighting a rock hard cock should be forced to see such perfect lips lick and suck those long, slender fingers clean.

"Enough!" he growled, dropping the corked brandy bottle with a thud onto the carriage floor. He reached for his wife, pulling her onto his lap.

Screaming from the sudden attack, Beth did not have a chance to fight back. Connie held her arms tight to her sides with one arm as his other hand lifted her skirts so that the only barriers between them was her drawers and his binding britches.

"Do not move," He whispered into her ear, licking back the saliva from his lips like a beast, before taking a quick nip of her neck.

Releasing Beth's arms, Connie won the struggle with his own clothes to finally release his throbbing member. With both hands, he grabbed Beth's drawers at the apex of her sex and tore the white linen in two, leaving the shredded remnants looped around each thigh. Gasping for air, Beth was silenced by shock and amazement by his warm sensual tongue on her neck. This will was week and she tasted like ambrosia.

She was stiff as a rod and trembled, in what he could only assume, was fear. His gentlemanly nature broke through for just a moment, forcing him to lean back and take into account of the woman in his arms. But logic and manner played in his favor when any argument began with "My wife."

"Relax, Wife," he instructed in a deep purr, "I will not take your maidenhead in a carriage, but if you think that I will fight my needs after such a show you have been giving me with those pies, you are greatly mistaken." Adjusting himself, he spread the beads of moisture at the tip of his cock and steel shaft before sliding his way up between the clenched globes of her ass. Guiding himself carefully to not breach either enticing entrance, he gave out a struggled breath of release as he felt the heavenly embrace of skin to skin.

"Please," her voice was weakened by fear, "I beseech you."

Kissing the side of her face, he leaned his forehead to the side of Beth's face and breathed in her scent, slowly trying to gain some control.

"You have nothing to fear of me wife, but if I do not find some release soon, I will not be able to wait till our wedding bed this night." One hand held the inside of one thigh, keeping her legs spread wide and he held her chin with his free hand turning her face to look over her shoulder and into his eyes. Dark and powerful, his eyes both frightened Beth and excited her.

Burning her with another kiss, she slowly submitted to him, melting into the embrace of his lips, but he needed so much more. Itching to touch her forbidden lips, Connie's fingers worked their way into the torn fabric and clamped on tightly to her treasure. She was warm and delightfully wet. His little virgin bride had her first taste of the forbidden, and Connie intended to help feed her the apple of his lust.

Sliding his fingers between her lips he breached her virgin passage, but left her maidenhead fully intact. Soft and warm, he began to imagine what a pleasure it would be once he had her properly prepared for him, when she is shaved and oiled. His fingers reached her precious barrier and he pulled back to avoid any risk of losing control and robbing him of her sacred gift. Running between the folds, he spread her perfumed juices over her sex. Her panting grew erratic until, at last, he pinched her bud between his fingers, sending her rear to jump up a bit, and clenching his cock all the tighter.

He pushed her lower-back away from him. Her perfect round globes gripped his sex tighter and pulled him into the crevices, only stopping with agonizing self-restraint to avoid entrance. "Sweet heaven." he exhaled, shaking from lust and guiding her with a firm grip on her inner thigh. Soon he had her moving in a quickening rhythm that followed his stroking fringes. Taking his wet fingers from her sex, he spread her juices over his stiff rod in one firm stroke.

"I can smell your sex," he whispered in her ear and Connie's body lost all ability of movement.

Printed in Great Britain
by Amazon